IT ONCE WAS

IT ONCE WAS

Jesse James Angelino

Edited by Rachel Amy Byrne
Photography by Zachary Coons

Columbus, Ohio

This book is a work of fiction. The names, characters and events in this book are the products of the author's imagination or are used fictitiously. Any similarity to real persons living or dead is coincidental and not intended by the author.

The views and opinions expressed in this book are solely those of the author and do not reflect the views or opinions of Gatekeeper Press. Gatekeeper Press is not to be held responsible for and expressly disclaims responsibility of the content herein.

IT ONCE WAS

Published by Gatekeeper Press

2167 Stringtown Rd, Suite 109

Columbus, OH 43123-2989

www.GatekeeperPress.com

Copyright © 2022 by Jesse James Angelino

All rights reserved. Neither this book, nor any parts within it may be sold or reproduced in any form or by any electronic or mechanical means, including information storage and retrieval systems, without permission in writing from the author. The only exception is by a reviewer, who may quote short excerpts in a review.

The cover design and editorial work for this book are entirely the product of the author. Gatekeeper Press did not participate in and is not responsible for any aspect of these elements.

Library of Congress Control Number: 2022936593

ISBN (paperback): 9781662927782

Contents

PREFACE	3
INTRODUCTION	5
1. CASING THE KANGAROO	7
2. THE NIGHT OF THE SCUM PANTHER	19
3. RIPPER VAN WINKLE	31
4. THE ISLAND OF ALEISTER CROWLEY	43
5. THE DEPRAVED GAMBIT'S OF THE ACHEAMPONG TWINS.	61
Part 1, The Morning Of (Jesse, 7AM)	64
Part 2, The morning of (Aliyah, 7AM)	67
Part 3, The afternoon of (Me and Aliyah, 12PM)	70
Part 4, The night of (Myself, Aliyah, Micah,Tony and Selena, 7PM)	71
6. THE CITY THAT NEVER SLEEPS (SO WHY SHOULD I?).	81
"THE END"	99
ACKNOWLEDGEMENTS	103

> *"When you are lost, it is always wise to return to where you started"*
>
> – *Ancient Chinese proverb*

Preface

HAVE YOU EVER OVERHEARD someone saying something juicy from another room?

Has anyone ever explained an expressive story that left you thinking to yourself "Alright, now I gotta know how this pans out?"

Or maybe you are like me and you listen to exchanges on podcasts so engaging that you feel like you are actually socializing.

Just a dog listening to the radio while your owner is out.

A good story can change you. If you're wondering how, look no further than silence.

Harvard studies can show us that listening to enticing subject matter can charm us and change the gray matter in our heads. The electrical impulses in our brain can increase and we get to score quick hits of all the "feel goods" such as cortisol, dopamine, oxytocin, and even endorphins! (This is why gossip is so much fun!)

During summer time as a child, my mother would take me to parties and barbecues at friends' homes where they would eat, drink, and share canards (some especially scandalous) late into the night. I would often find myself helplessly dropping eaves of these conversational tales more often than seeking entertainment via television. There wasn't really a program on the tube that I could find more captivating than a good real live story. Especially when it hit close to home, and as long as my mom and her friends would exchange them on those warm nights of yore, so would I pass on sleep for them.

Over the years I would eventually start dating. (Which is awesome if in this case you love to go over yarns back and forth over dinner which I do.)Talking to my dates let me find nostalgia in stories I was never a part of.

Good conversation used to be an art form and that's one of the biggest reasons I wanted to write all this. These days I see it less and less. Trying to catch up, discuss, bitch to, or reminisce these days is hard when all people seem to want to do in a social setting is look at their phones... or worse, have you look at their phones! You know the guy or girl who corners you to watch a youtube video they find entertaining while you refrain from the almost sexually strong urge to tap the screen and check the video length.

I have shot the shit from behind bar counters, on long car rides, at house parties, from in front of bar counters, around the water cooler at work, surrounding a campfire, shouting on a bar counter, and various podcasts for so long that when one of my friends told me to just "write the damn book already" I finally took them up on it. When I would podcast on East Hunter Radio a few years back, these comedic essays and narratives would draw a lot of positive feedback. However podcasts come and go, but books are forever and so here I am to document these funny stories for future generations and legacies.

Nary would a night out on the town, a hike into the great northern Catskills, a cross country jog, or even my first time ordering scungilli at a restaurant (An Italian favorite, it's a small mollusk that lives inside conch shells.) be undertaken without the idea that one day, This will amount to some fireside chat later on down the line at some holiday party where no one even knows me, achieving some kind of chintzy immortality.

Introduction

WELL, HERE I AM, 35 years old and finally getting around to writing this.

This (along with my sensational daughter Lily) may very well be the only legacy I will leave to this world. My stories.

You see, my father (God rest his soul.) was a brilliant musician who cut his teeth on the rock and roll scene of New York City during the 1980's. He worked very hard alongside the Local One stagehands out of the Beacon Theater to support myself and my mother while also building a presence in the music scene, purchasing recording studios all across the five boroughs, forming his own band "The F.R.O.N.T", and even replacing Billy "Diamond" Stiger in the Heavy Metal supergroup "Twisted Sister."

In addition to messing with the drums once every 100 years and constantly singing at social gatherings both apropos and not apropos, music didn't seem like it was going to be my calling. Making people laugh however, came a lot more naturally.

The manuscript of stories I have been talking about since my 24th birthday. Never really saw the point in owning scars if you are never gonna talk about them so here are all of mine laid bare for your comical amusement. The following is a collection of fictitious short stories and events.." Any similarity to actual persons, living or dead, or actual events, is purely coincidental. Each tale has been peppered with a generous dose of yellow journalism. Though I perceive you will find them nonetheless relatable. They are a list of events, both small and large, that I have managed to captivate small audiences with over the years in many social occasions from all walks of life, be it condo or crack house.

I am aware many of these stories will come across as easily avoidable disasters but I have long held the personal belief that your 30's are the best time to clean up the mess you made of your life during your 20's.

Hopefully you can lose yourself to these pages of trespassing in zoo's after dark, blood baiting sharks, stalking ghosts while high, breaking into Andy Warhol's secret party room below the streets of New York and much .... much more.

There is an old Arabian proverb that tells us that "There are four things that cannot be taken back." "The spoken word, the sped arrow, the past life and the neglected opportunity" I hope that's true. I don't want to have to take any of this back. I hope I can write something here that will axiomatically challenge all four of those pedagogy and bring the spotlight back to a new generation of comedians in the Catskills.

So pull up a beanbag, throw on some light jazz, and prepare to enter the terrifyingly beauteous world of Jesse "James" Angelino. (Sorry my intro was not directed by Ridley Scott and could have been longer.)

1

Casing the Kangaroo

A GOOD CROSS SECTION of people are always shocked when I tell them that I never got drunk before the age of 18. (Growing up in a quiet mountain town, I guess it's expected?) Let alone, amongst friends at this point. So maybe that's why it was so easy to get carried away with a remark I had made to my girlfriend of the time Bella, who had driven me to my job eight hours earlier that day. We were headed to a wine bar in Saugerties, NY where I worked called the "Lil Vouve", when we passed an enormous billboard that was advertising for the local zoo. It showed off giraffe's, alligators, tigers, and even elephants. Everyone from the area knew the place, and as far as I could tell, would visit it at least once every summer with their families.

The billboard was practically outside my Bella's house so I saw the thing almost every other day, but today as I looked out the passenger's side window of her Mitsubishi, I tried looking at it from the eyes of a tourist. I fixated on a kangaroo that was in the corner of one of the photos, rubbing its hands almost as if planning something.

"Have you ever noticed that?" I asked Bella.

"Noticed what?" she asked, trying to focus on the damn road.

"That kangaroo, it looks like it's up to something!" "Look at its hands!" She quickly glances into the driver's side mirror.

"What's...with his hands?" she asks.

I sat up from a slouch. "His hands!" "He's rubbing his hands, he looks like a smug prick!" "Someone should get that guy!" I continue.

Bella gives me a quick look. "Are you high right now?" (Pot)

"No" I lied to her as the subject fell and we moved on to something else. If only I had known the fate ahead of me sealed by that comment.

I didn't own a personal vehicle at this point in my life, (Fuck me, right?) so Bella would drive me to work and back most days. We both worked very close to one another so I would frequently go home with her as well. Especially if it was a Friday. (And it was a Friday.) That night when we got in from work, Bella's brother invited us to come down to the basement and have some beers with the guys. Bella tells me that she's super tired and just wants to grab some sleep before an early shift in the morning, but that since I had off the next day to go have some fun. I love beer so there's no arm twisting here. Before anyone can yell "Prost!" I already have an overpriced Irish stout in my hand that tastes like someone left a Yoo-hoo out for three days. Bella's brother Jimmy, was one of those guys that made being Irish his whole entire personality. Everywhere you looked in his room there were orange, white, and green flags, Guinness socks, and a standing hamper that was probably filled with potatoes for all I fucken knew. His two other buddies, Jake and Eli are also here tonight to play beer pong. (Or Beirut for those of you from New England that saw a game where balls drop into cups and thought "Kind of looks like planes dropping bombs on a city.") Jake is around my age, (Which at the time was 23) and probably the nicest guy I have ever met in my life. In fact he is probably TOO nice. I once watched Jake get stuck in a vein on his leg by an errant dart thrown by two guys playing "Cricket" in a bar. Jake pulled the dart out and apologized to the two guys for getting blood on it before washing it off with his own shirt and giving it back. I couldn't believe it.

Eli on the other hand was a year younger than us and a fucking psycho at the best of times. He loved two things above all else in the world. Gambling and performing dangerous stunts that could get him killed. Everyone in town used to talk about how Eli once led the local police force on a chase through two towns and only finally stopped because his Avenger ran out of gas.

So I guess I should not have been surprised when in a buzzed stupor I regaled about the smug kangaroo from earlier that somebody should "get" and Eli agreed. It's one of those tense moments when the laughter in the room dies down and everyone wonders "Is he serious?" "Is he is he serious?"

"No balls" Eli would say famously whenever he wanted to goad someone into joining him on one of his infamous escapades.

"You want to go up to the zoo right now and kidnap the kangaroo?" I asked red faced and laughing.

Eli looked at me like I got his order wrong at the drive-thru. "That's what I fucken said!" "We can walk, it's not even that far!" I can't stop myself from laughing some more in his face.

"Eli, I'm not worried about the predicate of what you just said, I meant what would we do with a kangaroo once we got one?" "Bring it back here!?" I jest.

Eli shrugs. "Yea I mean imagine the look on Bella's face in the morning when she comes downstairs and sees a god damn kangaroo, dude." "You'll be like...the coolest guy she ever dated"

I roll my eyes. "I would think so, but she won't."

Jimmy interjects, pickled as an evening bishop by this point. "Fuck it, I'm in and I live here." "I give full consent for the animals stay!"

I am actually wondering if this is going to happen at this point. Jake is even saying he will go if I agree to.

"You guys are insane!" I say. "How would we even do this?"

Eli walks over to a sack of potatoes lying on the washing machine (I told you) and dumps them all out into a laundry basket. He then holds the empty sack up to me in display. "I'll walk up and put it in a hold and you guys throw the sack over him." "That should work!"

I am shaking my head "That is fucking preposterous!" I yell. "We don't know how big it is!" "The sack might not fit!"

Jake is in the corner now also adding "I think I remember reading somewhere that those things can box really well too."

Jimmy hiccups. "Eli's dad was a professional boxer, I THINK he can take a kangaroo in a glove match."

"I'm thinking there won't be any gloves, Jim." I told him. Eli is now halfway out the door. "Are we doing this?"

Jimmy throws on a black hoodie and is already following Eli. Jake looks back to me. I stare at the three of them. I am very intoxicated. I am also 23 years old and really love making new friends.

* * *

THE TREK TO THE ZOO required walking up many hills in the dark outback of the Catskills. It was almost 1:30 in the morning though so we didn't really have to worry about any passing cars noticing us as we approached the open gates to the park. The four of us crouched like Hobbits amongst the brush, peering into the zoo's open field beset on both sides by various animal paddocks. In the distance there was a loud cawing from some exotic bird I did not recognize.

"Ok, obviously I have never been here at night." "Which exhibit has the kangaroo?" Jimmy asks. "None of us know that man..." Jake replies.

"Guess we'll just have to check 'em all" Eli whispers. That bird cawing is starting to get closer and louder.

"Fuck!" Eli whispers loudly, "I forgot the potato sack at the house!" I'm laughing again. "Oh no!" I mock him. "Not the most integral and realistic part of the plan!"

The darkness makes the animal enclosures impossible to identify from our position out in the woods. The only thing we can make out clear as day is one of the soda vending machines positioned against one of the main service buildings.

"ARACK!" we hear suddenly from behind us. The four of us whip around practically pissing ourselves in fear and panic to see a peacock staring back at us quizzically, its feathery plumage making it appear larger and more menacing at first. We pull ourselves together, but the peacock's earth shattering shrieks continue to unnerve us from this close. (Remember, this thing can be heard cawing from maybe 70 yards away so right up next to us is pretty annoying)

"What the hell does it want?" Jimmy asks.

"I don't know" I start to say, "But it's kind of drawing attention to us right now." "Attention we don't want if this is going to work."

Eli nods in agreement and tries menacing the peacock to see if it will run off in fright but it just raises its claw in response.

"Hahahahahahaha" Jake laughs. "It's calling you out, dude!"

Eli does not look amused. He finally goes to push the bird away but as soon as he bears down on it, the little guy gives chase into some nearby bushes, casting back at us it's awful chirp.

"You know..." Jimmy begins drunkenly. "I kind of remember Bella tried to tell me once about these guys letting that peacock roam around at night like some kind of guard dog." "I think that thing was trying to blow up our spot just now, the staff might know we are here already."

Eli looks wild eyed at Jimmy. "Are you being serious right now?' Jimmy smiles. "Why would I make something like that up?"

Eli stood up from his crouch. We all did. "Alright" he says. "We gotta move fast now, we'll search this exhibit first."

Eli uses one arm to hoist himself over a large wooden fence that reminds me of a corral. "Whoa whoa whoa..." I started protesting. "You actually want us to physically go INTO the exhibits to check them!?" "That's WAY fucking dangerous Eli!" "We know they have an alligator around here somewhere, what the hell would we do trapped in an enclosure with one of those, huh!?"

I missed it in the dark but now Jimmy is over the fence in the paddock as well with Eli already." "It's ok," Eli whispers. "I learned how you're supposed to wrestle an alligator when I still went to St. Rose College." "I got this" "If we shine our lights to look into the exhibits it will only give us away." He and Jimmy are now hightailing it further into the enclosure to investigate while I and Jake drunkenly climb the fence too. Jake is laughing and I am muttering "That's probably not true "

I and Jake are now inside of the exhibit with absolutely no idea what animal this is home to. (Smart kids, right?) We catch up to Eli and Jimmy who show us that this enclosure is for a herd of horses. One of the better looking specimens of which Eli was currently petting when we reunited. "Thank god" I whisper out loud. Jimmy starts laughing with Jake. I'm not sure about what but probably the very sight of the whole situation if I had to guess. Eli slowly takes his hand off the horse and starts crawling up the side of a hay bale right next to them. Once he has fully mounted the hay bale I see him attempt to swing one of his legs over the horse's back.

'ELI!" I do one of those whisper shouts your mom or your girlfriend does when you're embarrassing them in public. "WHAT THE FUCK ARE YOU DOING, YOU MANIAC!?"

Eli's leg is now on the horse and he is trying to use it to pull the rest of his body on to it. (WITHOUT A SADDLE) "ELI, PLEASE STOP!" I plead.

"It's ok!" Eli answers back. "I know how to ride horses bareback."

"What!?" I replied. "What the fuck does that have to do with the price of tea in China right now, why are you doing this?" "Please!' "I will give you $5 if you stop this right now!"

He isn't listening to me anymore. I can hear him continue, "Well...I watched my sister do it a million times growing up." (Remember we're very drunk) I don't know if Eli was able to actually mount the horse that night. It occurred to me years later after getting to know him better that this sort of behavior was a pretty standard exercise in pushing his luck to see how far it would go. (Hence the aforementioned gambling and dangerous stunts.)

What happened next was utter bedlam. In the dark I couldn't see what happened exactly, but what I can tell you, is that Eli's attempts to mount the horse were not welcomed. The horse tore away from him faster than Walt Flannigan's dog and broke into a heavy charge that must have spooked the other horses because in just a few seconds..... the four of us were smack in the middle of a fucking stampede.

As the four of us lost each other in the ensuing ebe of equine, I realized that if I hoped to survive this I would have to beeline to the fence before I was trampled to death. I'm already running.

The fence is too far. Fuck.

Plan B.

Through the adrenaline and the shadows I spot more hay bales. New plan. Climb up one one of those bad boys and start praying to God almighty that one of these beasts does not collide with one.

As horses gallop past me,(Frighteningly close) I can hear those intense Swahili pitches from the stampede scene in The Lion King where Simba is running for his life before his father dies blaring in my skull as I parkour my way atop the nearest hay bale and turn to see if my new friends are alive anymore.

No sign of Eli or Jimmy, BUT THERE'S JAKE! I see him! He sees me and notices what I have done. In mere seconds he understands and claws his way onto the closest hay bale to mine. We are two young men just standing on hay bales with terror stricken faces in the dark as the herd charges like the Rohirrim across the fields of the Pelennor all around us.

As quickly as the stampede started it was all over. Me and Jake came down from our hay bales and ran to meet one another.

"Where the fuck is Jimmy?" I ask. "And what happened to Eli?"

Jake shrugs. "Dude, I don't know, I was following you the whole time and did not look back once." He stares down at some cuts he has accumulated on his arms and hands.

"I think I got tetanus though?"

I am too distracted to figure out how he could have managed that. I watch as the last of the horses vanish from my field of vision.

"Someone will have heard all that" I tell Jake. "We gotta get out of here." He is already ahead of me and making his way back to the fence.

We arrive at it together and climb back over to actual safety.(For now) We decide to exit the park before figuring out what to do about Jimmy and Eli just in case the park's security came to check on the stampede. When we are outside of the gates to the park we resume our original huddle in the brush where we can see in but no one could spot us.

"Ok" I start to tell Jake. "How do we find them without getting caught?"

Before Jake can answer, he is instantly cut off by the loudest, most blood curdling, inhuman, guttural screech either of us have ever heard since.

We glance at each other, panic building with rapid success.

"What...the fuck...was that.... ?" (It doesn't even matter which one of us said this, we were so terrified) Jake is staring out into the wild dark, his eyes a pair of crazed Manson lamps. "BroI think....that was a fucking Wendigo my dude.......................... " he says.

My flight instinct is kicking in. "A what!?" I ask him.

"A Wendigo man." He continues. "A Native American spirit born from cannibalism." I'm dumbfounded.

"No..." I told him. "I think it's an animal." "It could be something crazy from inside the zoo...or worse...something from out here!"

Jake proceeds to tell me we need to keep moving. Get back to the house and find Bella and ask her for help. Luckily just then, Jimmy and Eli appeared from out of the woods to our right and rejoined us while laughing.

"THAT...was fuckin wild!" Eli chuckles.

"Are you guys ok!?" I ask them. "Where the hell were you?"

Jimmy is still yuking when he explains to me Eli fell off the horse and hurt his ass but they escaped behind the herd and over the back fence, out into the woods beyond the enclosure.

"Did you hear that scream a minute ago?" Jake starts with them. "What was that!?" Eli and Jimmy look confused. "We didn't hear a scream." Jimmy says.

"A scream like a person, were you guys spotted?"

"No!" I say. "Well...I don't think we were." "Either way, we are scrapping the kangaroo idea, I've had all the excitement I can manage for one night." "Time to go!"

Eli gazes forlorn back at the park. "All that and we have nothing to show for it!" he says.

Jimmy looks back into the park as well. "Well what if we run back in and at least buy a soda from the vending machine for us all to share on the walk back?" "That would be kind of cool."

I say nothing but everyone else agrees. To get to the vending machine we would have to walk across the park's main field. (Which has flood lights trained on them) Not to mention we would be doing this all AFTER the peacock and those horses gave away our presence.

Jake and Eli call "Not it". (Rare for Eli) so it's me and Bella's Brother Jimmy going to get the damn soda.

"Let's make this quick." I say as the two of us creep (as best as two men in a flood lit field can creep) up to the vending machine.

I pat myself down to show Jimmy I have no money on me while trying not to make much sound. He feels around in his pockets and fishes out the asking dollar and hands it to me. I feed the dollar to the machine and give a quick push on the "Sprite" button. Nothing.

"I don't believe it," I tell Jimmy. "After all that, the thing ate my fucking dollar!" Jimmy laughs. "You mean MY dollar, let's get out of here."

Again we pho creep back out to our companions near the gates and start the long walk back to Jimmy's.

"What a night!" I exclaimed to them.

The cell phone in my pocket is vibrating. (We all put ours on silent for this occasion because we are not COMPLETELY stupid, just mostly.)

I pull it out to look. Bella's name is scrawled across the tiny screen. My shook eyes peer over at the little clock in the corner. 3:44 AM.

"Fuck!" I yell. "Bella probably was wondering why the hell I never came to bed and went downstairs and saw all of us were gone!" "What am I gonna say to her!?" "She will never understand this!"

"Ugh!"

Jake throws a friendly arm around me. "Don't worry bud, if you're in trouble we are all in trouble." "Pick up the phone and I'll talk to her first, I've known Bella my entire life"

I hand him the small flip phone and he answers.

I can hear her asking questions, concerned, upset …… then angry.

Jake hands me the phone. "It's going to be alright bud, she just wants a word with you." I take back the phone. "No shit Scotland Yard, she called MY phone."

I answered her. "Hello?"

"Hey, yes hunny I am OK, we are ALL OK."

"Just took a walk up to the zoo since it was such a lovely night."

'Why?"

"To kidnap a kangaroo of course."

"A harmless jape, I promise"

"Oh, security would have shot us if they caught us?"

"How reckless"

"You are absolutely right, we the four of us are complete fucking idiots for pulling a stunt like this."

"I don't want to have to go back into the world of dating around here"

"Eli says the reason they call this place "Cats-kill" is because all of the pussy here is dead!" "Please don't break up with me over this."

"Yes, I agree I should have called or sent a text before worrying you." "Why didn't I?"

"Hunny, I really just didn't think that abducting marsupials was your bag."

CLICK

2

The Night of the Scum Panther

AS I MENTIONED PREVIOUSLY, I work out of a wine bar in upstate NY called "The Lil Vouve," and have for quite a lot of years. Though I have come and gone many times, trying new things out in the big bad world I can safely say that for 11 years I have always managed to find my way back to this place. The biggest factor to this establishment's charm is its eclectic staff. The people who run this place are a roulette of characters ranging in archetypes from polished, window dress debutante's to the sparing and thrifty salts of the earth. All of whom I call my friends, and if any of you are reading this just know that spending time with you all is my favorite way to earn a living.

The bar's only male employee's was a triumvirate of fellas, including myself and two local guys that I go as far back as elementary school with. Connor and Klaus.

Connor had all the physical qualities of some back alley tough that used brute force to collect vig's for a loan shark. He was big, brawny and dressed like a Brooklyn dock worker. But past all that aesthetic he was one of the nicest and gentlest hands we had working in the place. Not really a fan of social settings he seemed to dread the idea of other people so much I would often joke that his ideal job would have been a lighthouse keeper…in the Yukon. Still, he always got along with me famously and always has since the fourth grade. Knowing all this, I can begin telling you that Klaus was the antithesis of everything Connor was or is. He was a consistent social butterfly that was great with our customers and even better with our staff. In high school he was well liked and was no stranger to our town's nightlife or entertaining guests in his home. (Which for irony's sake he shared with Connor.)

However…Once he had imbibed to a certain extent, (The amount is frighteningly fluctuant) Klaus's friendly personality could be usurped and replaced with a legalese speaking iconoclast that lived for conflict like a Spartan for war. We called this opposing personality "The Scum Panther." A character I have seen up close on a few occasions but none as memorable as the first.

Going out on a Friday night is a zeitgeist in your 20's , so when I received a text at work from my good buddy Lucas detailing a get together at one of the local German resorts for a night out I knew I was set. I was getting ready to close the bar up with Connor and Klaus when the latter invited me to a quick round if I was able to give him a ride to a spot in town for his own night out. Dave's Coffee House was not a misnomer. The place opened early with a café setting and closed as a tavern late at night.

I agreed and as always we extended an invitation to Connor who declined, much preferring the solitude of his books to a bar hop. Once the Lil Vouve was locked up nice and tight and all the stools were tableside, myself and Klaus hopped into my 2002 Hyundai Accent and steamed over to the corner of Partition and Main in Saugerties.

I was surprised to get a good spot that wasn't far from the venue. The inside was a sensory explosion from the quiet end of the day mindset back at Vouve. There was a live band inside playing folk metal.

The scene was a clash of local kids and older Woodstock guys that nurse IPA's while they describe the taste to you or drone on about "these records" or this "live show." It was my first time here so I followed Klaus to the bar where he ordered us a beer each. I had forgotten
our deal and ordered a glass of Cabernet as soon as he stepped off the line and wound up with both. (Not a bad look.) Klaus buys a bottle of red wine for us to split after we finish these as he abhors waiting in lines. I checked my phone and saw that it was almost time to head to my next destination. I thanked Klaus for the drink and informed him that it was "on to the next one".

It was then that Klaus surprised me by asking if he could come along. Klaus had never asked to hang out with my friends from outside of work before so I was a little shocked. "Sure!" I told him. "We're getting together in Cairo at the Riedlbauer's German resort!" He has no idea where the place is or what kind of venue it caters to but is excited nonetheless to try something new. The drive out there understandably begins to concern him once we take to the back roads that lead up to the resort. "I should have mentioned it before." "This place is kind of in the middle of nowhere!" I yell to him as we both urinate simultaneously on opposite sides of the road where my parked car provides light to see where we are aiming.

Once we arrive at the resort I begin the introductions. "Lucas, this is my coworker Klaus, Klaus my buddy Lucas." I start. Lucas is a jock that always looks like he is about to turn into a werewolf but still nice enough. He shakes Klaus's hand and introduces another mutual, Manny. I had met Manny a few times but we were never very close. All I could remember of the guy was that he was very into technological advances of late and had been jailed once for deserting the
U.S. Army.

It was time to show Klaus the lay of the land. There was a certain feeling of pride showing off one of my favorite watering holes to newcomers who had not realized its existence outside of town. Riedlbauer's is a beautiful place. To date I have had a lot of really great memories there. It mostly serves as an inn with its own bar but the township of Cairo remains so small and intimate that getting drunk at a hotel you don't have a room at is considered fine. The inside had high ceilings, old fireplaces, a dance floor with DJ's playing new hits, (or sometimes polka.) a pool table and of course the bar. We settled in and immediately Klaus asked what was good here. "This is a German resort." I told him. "So you better drink as the Germans do..." I order us two 35 ounce steins of the Fatherland's best here. Klaus is over the moon to receive this much beer without having to wait in line. We cheers and started downing. A few seconds in Klaus stops and lowers his glass with a disgusted look. "Bro... what is this?" "This is not beer my dude." He says.

"What do you mean?" I ask. "I drink this stuff all the time, it is great!"

Klaus puts his stein down. "Jesse, this might look like beer but it tastes like fucking BLOOD!" I approach and take a swig of his drink. It's the same as mine and I can't detect anything wrong with it.

"Ok..." I begin to say. "I guess you are not a fan of German brews, that's fine." "We can get you something else."

"Yeah, I can't enjoy anything that reminds me of rust, I think I am going to just order some White Russians" he answers back before heading over to the bar. The bartender is a girl I have known for years named Petra and she is extremely easy on the eyes, very playful, but takes no shit from anyone. Especially at her job. Klaus gets her attention and starts ordering twin White Russians to double fist and notices a bell hanging near the corner of the ceiling for the wrap around bar. "Hey, what's this?" He utters while reaching up to ring the bell. I realize what he is doing too late to stop him and the chimes sound out through the room, getting everyone's attention. "What's everybody smiling about?" he asks as I arrive at his side. "By ringing that bell you have just agreed to buy everyone in here a round of drinks!" I told him. His demeanor turns to annoyed confusion. "Why the fuck would I do that?" "This is a stupid bell!" he starts to bitch. "It's for like, guys who just proposed to a girl who said yes, or an announcement someone is having a baby, stuff like that!" "All these people think you are getting them booze now!" I answered him.

"Fuck that!" Klaus starts. "They should have a sign or something to explain that." "Kind of seems like robbery to me man." "I don't really have the money to buy drinks for everyone here."

Petra is now standing in front of us as expected. Her foxy deutsch features quickly changing Klaus's mind regarding the tradition of the inn's bell. "You buying all these nice people a round?" She asks with a smile. Klaus reluctantly agrees that he will purchase everyone in the room a Kamikaze each. He had secretly hoped that narrowing down the drink options would deter any takers. But these were Germans, and I watched as each one, including Lucas, Manny, Myself, and even Petra the bartender graciously accepted their surprise beveridge's much to Klaus's chagrin.

Klaus's bitterness about his now large tab was awakening the panther inside, but I could not have known.

An older gentleman on one of those electronic Rascals for getting around, invited Klaus over to where he and his friends were sitting to thank him for the drinks. While over there, I lost track of Klaus to chat with Lucas, Manny, and Petra, figuring he would be alright on his own. I turned out to be right. A short while later he returned to us in a much better mood with the Rascal guy in tow.

"Guys!" Klaus began. "This here is Louis!" "He's a retired cop with the Bronx PD and he told me he can get me in on a ride along and see some real shit!" "This is my boy now!" Klaus takes his hand with Louis's in one of those locked handshakes and is now roaring with the inevitable laugh of the wasted.

Klause: "Louis, this here is my buddy Jesse." "Boy is he a fun guy!" "Type of dude who starts the conga line, ya know what Im sayin?

"Louise moves to shake my hand and I accept.

"Hey Jesse, what's this!?" He yells, plunging his hand into some small cubbies individualized to different sections of the bar. I had never noticed them before. He produces a green muppet from the second one he tries and immediately puts it on his head like a hat. "I don't know what the fuck is going on in this place, but now I have a puppet hat!"

The puppet was some sort of friendly looking green monster with stringy hair whose bottom opening was probably so someone could operate the puppet with their hand but Klaus had somehow stretched it out to fit over his entire head. The entire bar is filled with laughter and people smiling and pointing at Klaus's hijinks. Which is why this next part is so awful. Klaus has finished all his booze and is now running low on cash because of the bell. He comes over to me (with the puppet still on his head) and asks me if I have any pot.

Me: "I did not bring any with me tonight, no."

Klaus: "Well, I kind of want to get high and I am almost out of money because of your weird fucking bell for rich people or whatever so do you think someone could smoke me up real quick?"

Me: "Lucas might be able to get you some, but the rest of these people are all seniors vacationing up here from the city so I wouldn't try asking any of them."

Klaus: "Well what about that hot bartender?" "She looks like she gets high." Me: "She doesn't, don't ask Petra." "I will talk to Lucas."

Klaus: "Not your friend!" "I was talking about the other one, Afro-dite over there."

He points at a lovely dark-skinned girl that has stopped to chat with Petra behind the bar and does in fact have an afro.

Me: "I don't know who that is but please do not ask the only black girl here if she any pot PLEASE KLAUS"

Klaus ignores me and beelines back to the bar (Still with the puppet on his head) and asks Petra if someone here will get him high. The Panther has already awoken. Petra's response is laughter followed by her explaining how she does not smoke habitually and doubts most of her clientele do either.

Afro-dite leaves after hearing this.

Klaus, now fucked-in-half drunk turns to address the room.

Klaus: "You all know me, I hooked you all up with those sweet Kaze's and now all I want is….it would be really cool…if someone got me high." "RIGHT NOW"

He is holding on to the bar like he's in some sort of earthquake. Like it's a lifeline. I can see Petra getting angry. She knows that this is not the crowd for such behavior, and Klaus is only getting worse.

Klaus: "Will somebody PLEASE, just fucking get me high!" "How is it that nobody here smokes?" Petra turns to me.

Petra: "I think your friend has had enough, it might be time to leave."

I quickly finish what's left of my drink and am ready to get Klaus out of here but before I can stop him, he is already recklessly grabbing cash from Petra's tip jar and counting it out so he has whatever it is that he spent before the bell incident.(Still with the puppet on his head.) Petra's eyes are now consumed with fury for Klaus.

Lucas has finally stepped in and is now confronting the Scum Panther to calm down. The wolf and the panther clash.

Lucas: "Look man, I don't want any problems…but you got to give that money back to my friend here or there is going to be some"

He gestures to Petra, who might as well be levitating in an aura of flames by now. Klaus turns back to Lucas.

Klaus: "Will you get me high?" Lucas shakes his head.

Lucas: "This is a resort man, no one here has any weed." "I'm sure if you just go with Jesse right now though, he can take you to some." Klaus returns Petra's tip money to the jar.

Klaus: "I AM NOT GOING ANYWHERE UNTIL SOMEONE FUCKING GETS ME HIGH!"

Myself and Lucas escort Klaus out into the parking lot. (Still with the puppet on his head.) I start my car and we make our way back out towards Saugerties.

In order to return Klaus to his home, I would have to bring him all the way out to his parents' place in Glasco, south of Saugerties. Not exactly close to the heart of Greene County where we had just departed from, nor anywhere near any of my normal routes home and the panther's claws were still out. As I stare at the neon green digits that read "1:32 AM" across my dash's clock, Klaus begins to fumble for his cell phone in the dark of my passenger's seat. He calls his girlfriend Mary, but a guy answers.(The puppet is gone now, but to where?)

Klaus: "Mary?" "Who is this?" "Well, Can you put Mary on?" "Well, I didn't call your phone, I called hers so how bout you give her the phone?" "Don't talk to you like what?" "OH, YOU'RE GOING TO KICK MY ASS?" "WELL FUCKIN DO IT BRO" "WHERE ARE YOU?" "POUGHKEEPSIE!?" "WORD, WELL MY BUDDY IS DRIVING ME HOME SO MAYBE YOU CAN MEET ME AT MY HOUSE AND BEAT ME UP?"

"COME TO MY HOUSE, MY ADDRESS IS 2286 SEYLER TERRACE!" "YOU CAN SHOW UP ANYTIME YOU WANT AND BEAT ME UP IN FRONT OF MY MOM WHO IS DYING OF CANCER!"

He shouts and waves his arms around like an angry Grand Theft Auto character. This sort of thing will attract unwanted attention from

Johnny Law and in case you missed some reading I have been drinking. (I know, I know. Drinking and driving is bad but I thought I would have had more time to sober up before we wound up here.)

Me: "Klaus, you should see yourself right now, hang up the phone!" My words don't reach the panther.

Klaus: "...EVEN BETTER!" "WHY DON'T YOU SHOW UP TO MY JOB IN THE OLD GRAND UNION AND JAMESWAY PLAZA AND BEAT ME UP WHILE I'M WORKING!?" "COME SLAP ME AROUND IN FRONT OF MY BOSS AND CO-WORKERS AT THE FUCKING VOUVE!!!!!"

I need to ditch Klaus somewhere so he can sober up or I am going to jail tonight. My car winds down Bogart road into Palenville. PALENVILLE! THAT'S IT! I"ll just leave him at Jake's! (See Chapter 1.) Jake is the nicest guy in the whole Hudson Valley!" "He can't say no.

Jake: "Yeah, there is no fucking way you are bringing Klaus into this apartment in THAT state my dude, big sorry."

Jake turns back to his TV where he is watching old reruns of Buffy the Vampire Slayer.

Me: "C'mon man!" "This kid has no cap right now" "He's going to get me arrested if I try to drive him any further!"

Klaus is still yelling into his phone in the background. He has finally managed to get Mary on the line.

Klaus: ".....OK, I THINK I AM GETTING THE HANG OF THIS NOW MARY." "SO WHEN A MAN LIES TO A WOMAN IT'S "GASLIGHTING" BUT WHEN A WOMAN LIES TO A WOMAN ITS "ASTROLOGY.""

I turn back to Jake.

Jake: "Yea, definitely not man, besides my dad hearing all this from next door, I personally don't want to deal with this all night."

Me: "Fine!" "I'll get him out of here!" "Klaus let's go!"

* * *

BACK IN THE CAR, I decide it will be easier just to take Klaus home with me. This will cut down on my driving and there are more back roads to my house than his. The rest of the drive home, Klaus shares with me how many bullets he believes you would realistically need to kill Clifford the big red dog when he is not enquiring about weed. We get in at 2:30.

Luckily my sister Layla is throwing some sort of a party in the basement that is winding down but still rife with stoners. Klaus makes himself at home with my sister's friends and appears to calm down. As they smoke him up he talks to them about music and it almost seems as if the Scum Panther has gone back into the deep and angry recesses of Klaus's subconscious until the next time.

Everything appears to be going well and Klaus is higher than a Russian heating bill. I start ascending the stairs ready to resign myself to my room for the night when shortly after I hear that same raised voice return from earlier in the night to haunt me one last time. I stop and swing back to see Klaus menacing a scrawny "beard" with a band shirt and gauges in skinny jeans.

I charge back down knowing my sister and her friends stand no chance against the Panther.

Klaus: "....Yea, well I know a bitch when I see one and anyone who says Anthrax is a good band definitely closes the refrigerator door with his hips if you know what I mean."

BEARD: "At least I don't listen to bullshit like Within the Ruins you googly-eyed Elvis lookin fuck!"

Klaus lunges before I can intervene and the two toss each other around on the floor, rolling towards my woodstove. There is a break in the struggle where I notice Klaus has inserted his thumbs into the Beard's gauges.

Klaus now looking up at me: "Get this guy the fuck away from me Jesse or so help me GOD, I will rip this kids god damn ears off!" "I am SO SERIOUS"

I try to come between them, but the Beard uses the moment that Klaus looked up at me to sucker punch his head into the cast iron wood stove.

I managed to pull them apart.

Me: "Alright, everyone out!" "You don't have to go home but you can't stay in the basement!" "Let's go!" "Out!"

I bring Klaus to the living room where I lay him down on the couch. He holds the site of his recent injury while bitching about the pain. We put some ice on it and stay up for a bit just to make sure he's not concussed before finally calling it.

It has been 11 years since that night and though I am sure the Scum Panther has emerged by and by, I have been fortunate enough to see less and less of it.

A few years after that night, Klaus invited me over to his apartment in the village for a "Mexican Night" at his house, with promises of tacos, taquitos, and margaritas. It was the end of our shift and all I wanted to do was go home and sleep, but he guilt tripped me by telling me he had already purchased 4 sombreros for the occasion and now it looked like he was sadly going to have to wear them all, so I conceded.

That night at Klause's, he told me that he has been practicing boxing with his virtual reality headset once a week since the incident, buffing for a rematch against the nerfed beard that wronged him so.

3

Ripper Van Winkle

MEET MY GOOD FRIEND, Christian! Christian is a gangling Norwegian man from Cairo, NY whose hobbies include hiking, paraphrasing Jesuits, avid gaming, recreational marijuana use, being superstitious enough to believe in some mega cooked shit, and a predilection for being a real devil with the ladies. In 2009, Christian was able to have a calendar made with a Miss January-December of his sexual conquests just for that year alone with room for 2010 as well. We met at a house party he was hosting to celebrate his name day that Bella and Jake invited me to. Jake introduced us over a game of Kings.

Christian: "The card is categories, and the category I choose is... famous porn stars!" "I'll start with Sasha Grey" "New guy, you're up next!"

Me: "Uhhhhh, Jesse Jane!"

Christian: "Awesome!" "Jake, who do you got?" Jake: "Myself"

Christian: "No, you are out." "And stop drinking all my birthday beer!"

Jake: "Ya cheap bastad!" "Ya probably bought this 12 pack by following around the Boondock Saints and stealin the pennies from their victims eyes!"

* * *

EVER SINCE THAT NIGHT we have been excellent chums. Christian's mind worked in a very robotic fashion that demanded the sensical atmosphere my very presence abolished. It makes us a good team.

One of my favorite past times would be to draw him into an argument of the utmost foolishness, presenting it as candor to an audience while his Vulcan mind would attempt to use Turabian style citations to prove what was obviously wrong.

I could be at a gathering addressing a group as thus.

Me: "Curious that nobody talks about the origins of ranch dressing, which was patented by the late German scientist Dr. Josef Mengele." "That "Hidden valley" refers to the mass grave discovered in the Caucasus Mountains where ranch dressing was first used on a camp of Soviet POWs."

Christian: "That couldn't possibly be true." Me: "....And yet it is Christian" "And yet it is..."

Christian: "The war ended in 1945 Jesse!" "Dr. Mengele would have fled to Argentina by this time, at which point the honorable Steve Henson and his wife Gayle were patenting the recipe for ranch dressing 6, 177 miles away in Santa Barbara, California!" "False speech I name you!" Me: "You should double check Christian" "Imagine the egg on your face if I turn out to be right about this."

Christian: "No!" "I don't have to check!" "What you are saying is utterly ridiculous!"

So on and so forth. You get the picture of how our dynamic works.

Now I can tell you the story of how the both of us were harrowed into a situation involving the supernatural and eventually...a murder investigation.

On Christians thirty-fourth birthday, almost a decade now from the day we met, he invited me on a two day hike through the Sundown Wild

Forest in southern Ulster County, NY. During the hike we were supposed to scale a few of the Catskill Mountains we had yet to visit which was promising for aspiring Catskill 35'rs such as ourselves and so I agreed. The path would start us in Phoenicia, then onward over the Sundown and across three separate peaks before relinquishing us to Peekamoose Road at the end.

Christian had made a pivotal note of a lean-to located along the way, only a short distance off the trail we were taking and decided that it would be the perfect spot for our camp after nightfall. I was all for skipping the weight of a tent on a journey such as this and could not have agreed more.

With the plans set, I loaded my pack and early morning on the day of, my girlfriend Ames drove me out to the trailhead where I would be meeting Christian in Phoenicia.

Ames is one of the smartest girls I have ever met, and she dresses like Gwen Stacey does in the newer Spider Man comics, which I always thought was really hot. She was my blonde voice of reason with an entire bibliography of impressive accolades, both academic and recreational, to back up why I prioritized her counsel.

Christian ran late, and Ames had a long drive back to Oneonta so we said our goodbyes and she left me to wait on him at the root of the trail. Christian arrived shortly thereafter and we began the trek. The hike itself took us on a route through the Blue Mountains where modicums of time were spent gazing on the Hudson River below, or marveling at the Allegheny Highlands above. At long last we arrived at the mini-trail to the lean-to nearly four hours of me humming the Lord of the Rings theme later.

The sun had dipped low behind Slide Mountain and we were set in pitch dark.

As we approached the clearing where Christian had said the lean-to was, we began to hear sounds up ahead, almost like a party at first.

Me: "I guess someone else beat us there." "That sucks, now we'll have to share the campsite." "Oh well, maybe I can lure you into an argument about how I can prove the Grinch is Bosnian and we'll get some laughs."

Christian is not discouraged though and leads us on, though the closer we approach the more the sounds from the lean-to seem to morph and change.

What originally sounded like a gathering of many was now more like someone reprimanding their dog for wandering off. Like they were calling it back to the site.

Still we carried on until we stood in the clearing in front of one of the greatest unsolved mysteries of our time.

There was no fire, no people, no light whatsoever. Just a grassy meadow in inky darkness beset by a crude wooden lean-to, more than big enough for both me and Christian to sleep in.

But the noises from earlier could still be heard.

It was a man's voice. Loud now that we had entered the clearing.

The source came from a nearby cliff that overlooked a small ravine to the left of the campsite. Mysterious Voice: "1......0.....0...0...0....1!" "0....0.....0......0.....0.....1!" "1...0!" "1!'

Me: "Whaaaaaaaaat the fuck is that?"

Christian: "Why does he not have a flashlight?" "He also seems to either be unaware of or is completely ignoring our presence." "Odd, as we have made the appropriate designations of sound in order to politely announce ourselves." "It also seems as if he is communicating in Binary code..."

Mysterious Voice: "BLUE ALWAYS WINS!" "ALWAYS WINS!" "BLUE IS UNION!"

Me: "........."

Christian: "I'm going to go try to talk to him."

Me: "Christian, forget it." "Somethings not right about this guy, let's get out of here." "Now."

Christian ignores me and starts towards the voice on the cliff.

Mysterious Voice: "IN THE SHADOWS IS WHERE WE WILL SLEEP." "THIS WHOLE VALLEY IS ALWAYS IN SHADOW" "IN THE SHADOWS IS WHERE WE WILL AWAKE IN ONE YEAR FROM THIS NIGHT!" "THE WORLD WILL BE DIFFERENT THEN!!!!!"

Me: "CHRISTAN!" "DON'T YOU DARE GO NEAR THAT FUCKING GUY!" "IM WARNING YOU!"

Christian is almost within striking distance of the strange menace on the cliff when suddenly he stops dead in his tracks at the voice's command.

Mysterious Voice: "STEP BACK!!!!!!!!!!!!!!"

I creep as cautiously as I can to Christians side.

Me: "Time to go buddy, I am NOT going to sleep here with that guy around."

Christian: "Before we do anything hasty, let us smoke a bowl first and see if maybe he will move on from here now that he has company." "I require rest Jesse" "I am exhausted and we have traveled so far..."

I retrieve my flashlight from my bag and shine the beam towards the mysterious voice revealing a stark naked man, probably in his late forties. He has long filthy dark hair that flows down to his bare behind, which is matted in wet earth and leaves.

He stands at the very edge of the cliff, facing into the charcoal briquette of the night. Arms raised high above his head as if pleading to God on high, once more baying his strange Tibetan Numerology chants.

Me: "Are you not scared yet?" Christian: " "

Me: "Christian!?"

Christian: "All right....this is pretty fucked up actually." "We should leave at once."

We both steal away back into the eventide of the woodland realm with slowly erupting urgency, only stopping once we are standing on an all-encompassing rock face shaken up from the ground below.

Me: "Where is the nearest trailhead?" "We need an exit FAST!"

Christian: 'This will require an alteration to our route I did not anticipate." "I will need time adjusting to the new course."

Me: "Yeah well, make it Planck Time, because we don't have much of it."

"I'm calling Ames to tell her what's going on and where we are in case something happens."

I pull out my phone.

Me: "As soon as you know where we are going, tell me so I can relay it to her so she knows our heading and how long it should take us to reach it."

Christian is already analyzing a map of the Catskills he's had since before I knew him. I punch in my phone's passcode and dial Ames.

83.7 miles away in Oneonta, NY, Ames's phone starts to ring.

* * *

AMES IS A SUPERVISOR for a home where special needs adults live in West Oneonta. Her job requires her to constantly monitor not only the five men in her care, but the staff under her as well. Combine that with a shit load of computer data entry and you got yourself a girl that is not going to pick up on the first ring. She sits cozy at a large wooden table that looks like it was inexplicably torn from the "The Last Supper" while punching away on a keyboard. In her peripheral is a glowing brick with my name on it. She answers finally, taking a moment to hear what I have to say in a wildly inverted setting to my circumstance. She calmly received my tale while pacing about the warm and brightly lit main room of the house while running her hands occasionally over its impressive furnishings while I raved and shivered in the dark wilderness.

Ames: "Hello?"

Me: "AMES!" "I NEED YOU TO LISTEN TO ME!" "WE ARE IN A BAD WAY HERE!"

Ames: "What's wrong?" "Are you alright?"

Me: "For just the moment, myself and Christain have wandered into a kafkaesque situation out here and we need to leave immediately." "These woods aren't safe tonight."

Ames: "Where are you going?"

Right on cue, Christian approaches with his flashlight directing my attention to a nearby trailhead we can use as an exit in the town of Sundown on the map.

Me:"Were headed for the trailhead in Sundown!" "After that we will have to find a way back to Dan's car in Phoenicia."

Ames: "That's ridiculous Jesse, you guys walked all day." "You're not going to backtrack this late at night, I'm going to call the police."

Me: "NO!" "NO,DON'T DO THAT!" "CHRISTIANS BACKPACK IS COMPLETELY FILLED TO THE BRIM WITH WEED!"

Ames: 'I don't care Jesse, this sounds serious."

Me: "Ames please!" "MADONE!" "THEY'LL LOCK US BOTH UP JUST AS SOON AS RESCUE US!"

Just then, as if to dramatic irony, the rising scream of a man who sounds as if he is burning alive erupts like an air raid siren throughout the entire mountain range. Myself and Christian spin to face the woods from whence we just came, the source of the atomic bellow we had just heard. It was him, the lunatic from the lean-to. Ripper Van Winkle, and he was coming.

    Ames: "THAT'S IT!" "IM CALLING THE FUCKING COPS!"

    My phone's light goes idle as the call ends.

    My terror mounting, Christian stashes the map into his pack with matching alarm.

    Christian: "Adjournment Sine Die..."

* * *

I DON'T REMEMBER ANY sound as we streaked through the blackened wood, the adrenaline saw to that. Definitely something John Carpenter's synthesizer would score.

    We moved swiftly and robotically, never turning our heads, not even to look back. Our survival instincts had made us a pair of life preserving drones, but eventually I could not ignore the strange orb of bright light that seemed cracked amidst the rush of the passing tree's like a Dyson Sphere keeping parallel to our insane pace. Christian and I come to a clumsy halt and steal ourselves to the brush in order to avoid contact with the orb that is rushing to intercept us ahead at a bifurcation in the trail.

    Christain: "Look!" "A light!" "We may request assistance!" I pull the antsy fool back.

    Me: Could be help...could be a visionary killer." "We have no idea and I don't want to meet anyone else out in these woods tonight!" "Shut your fucking mouth and stay still till it passes" Christians immunity to my paranoia grants him strength enough to pull away from me and stand up fully.

    Christian: "HELLO!" He yells to the orb.

The orb comes to a sudden stop.

It slowly shines it's beam at Christan.

He stands in its rays like a victim of Archimedes fabled burning mirror for a few moments before the light vanishes instantly.

I observe as Christians rational mind struggles to understand what is happening before he says some of the dumbest shit I have ever heard.

Christian: "Jesse, I do believe the phenomenon we have just witnessed here was what the ancient celts describes as an "Ignis Fatuus." "A will-o-the-wisp."

I can't believe this.

Me:" You think apart from the madman chasing us right now that we are also being pursued by fairies!?" "Give me that backpack of weed, you're finished!"

I reach for his pack but he playfully shoves me away while laughing. Me: "Fine, keep your bud." "It would only slow me down anyway."

"For the sake of my sanity right now I'm going to pretend that light was another hiker who is just as afraid of us as we are of them, and killed the light to avoid us like we did to them before you decided to make like you were the fucking Philadelphia lawyer and yell to it."

Christian: "That conclusion is unlikely." Me:"Are you not scared enough!?" "Can we go!?"

Another half-hour's worth of blistering pace brings us to the trailhead and out onto a backroad outside the village of Sundown where a police cruiser is waiting for us. The officer is a young woman who steps out of her car and approaches us with a pad for reports. Christian looks shook. He's got a jungle in his backpack and is wondering if he's about to spend his birthday in jail.

Officer: "Which one of you is Jesse?" Me: "That'd be me."

Officer: "Your girlfriend contacted us, said you boys were being pursued by a crazy man."

We tell her everything.

Officer: "Alright, we're sending three rangers up there to investigate now." "Let's get you boys home."

It was a long drive back to Christain's vehicle in Phoenicia but the important thing was that we spent the rest of Christains birthday in the backseat of a cop car as God had intended.

Once we got back to my house in Saugerties (without incident from the gigantic backpack of marijuana Christain was hauling around in the police cruiser) and went to bed I thought the adventure was over.

But I was wrong...

* * *

TWO DAYS LATER I was staying at Ames's apartment in Oneonta when I received a call in the middle of the afternoon while cleaning. It was the police.

They informed me that myself and Christain might need to come in for questioning regarding a missing person's report out in that area.

Apparently, a 46 year old music teacher from Queens named Keith Johnson had disappeared somewhere near the same mountain, the same forest, the same trail and on exactly the same night as myself and Christain had been out there.

He could not be reached by phone and never checked in with his sister like he was supposed to after making camp. The police were now wondering if the strange man we had encountered at the lean-to and this missing person were connected somehow and since we were the only other people that were on the trails registry for that day we had become person's of interest in the case.

The rangers who headed the follow up investigation at the lean to that night described in their reports that they had found absolutely nothing at the campsite, making myself and Christan quite possibly the last two people to have ever seen that man.

I retold the story to the officer on the phone and he told me "Not to go too far" in the next couple of days. He concluded our interview by asking for Christains phone number so he could contact him but never reached out.

Not that it mattered much, because in another two days the police would find the body of the missing Keith Johnson dead in the forest outside of Shandaken, NY.

To this day it is unclear how or why he died. As I write this, the investigation is still ongoing but foul play was ruled out, so me and Christain never heard from the cops about it again.

News 4 New York reported that the missing man had no history of mental illness or substance abuse but had acted very suspicious in the days leading up to his disappearance. His students described him as uncharacteristically irritable and moody the last day they saw him at P.S. 29. I have often speculated that Ripper Van Winkle and the missing Keith Johnson may have been the same person post some unforeseeable mental breakdown out in the wilds but I guess I'll never know.

What I do know is that the Sundown Wild Forest where all of this went down is a real hotspot for weird shit. While following the case in the papers and online I came to discover that those woods used to host bizarre cults that worship old gods like Marduk and Lucifer for many years.

An allegedly cursed doll known as "The Crone Of The Catskills" was recovered from a cave in the Sundown by a pair of young men who ended up selling it to the Traveling Museum of the Paranormal and the occult" after its presence introduced a litany of sinister and unsettling events in each of their respective homes.

I could go on and on about all the odd and frightening occurrences that transpire in those dark hills but this next chapter will keep us plenty in the macabre as it is...

The Island Of Aleister Crowley

UPON THE HUDSON RIVER, just off the shores of Dutchess County is the island of Esopus. Bearing the appearance of what some might think at first glance is a petrified whale moored out on the tides by Staatsburgh, NY, this 1,500 foot long floating forest was once the home of the Esopus Tribe of the Lenape Indian Nation who protected the sacred monoliths they built there from Jesuit missionaries with death.

Fast forward to the Revolutionary war and this island is where His Majesty King George's navy lay encamped during the burning of our state's former capital, Kingston.

Then at last in 1918, the island was visited by the wickedest man in the world himself. Aleister Crowley. Famous occultist and alleged anti-christ, the beast who's dark rituals were to bring about the end of the world. It was here that Crowley made his home for quite some time, living betwixt the stony shores and eastern redbuds of the island while practicing meditation, translating the Tao Te Ching into English, and painting mysterious red markings across the giant rocks that surrounded the island. Pretty interesting right? I thought so too, and figured it warranted a visit. I owned my own kayak so getting there would be fun and easy.... or so I thought.

Enter William and Airy. A recently married couple that I had met over a game of "Sorry" at the Crossroads brewery in Catskill. William was a local man who had grown up on nearby Embought road while Airy was a transplant to our dear town from Tampa Bay, Florida.

William was lighthearted and charismatic. He was a realtor who enjoyed hallucinogens and going LARPING. His better half was a bubbly yet focused woman who worked as a maid to rich magnates so she could afford antique firearms.(I did say she was from Florida, didn't I?.) If I was going to the island of a former prophet of the shadows, then these were the two that I wanted to go with. We had made plans that involved me spending the night at their house so we could all get an early start south in the morning but I got caught up entertaining some gas station drunk and lost the night.

I still woke up as early as I could. I opened my eyes and grabbed my phone from the writing desk beside the bed. It was 11:30 in the morning. Shit. They definitely would have left by now. When I had told William that the founder of the Thelema religion "Hermetic Order Of The Golden Dawn" had lived on a mysterious island right in our backyard he could hardly wait another moment to get out there and trace whatever former steps that evil mystic had walked when he called that island home.

I called Williams' phone. He picks up and tells me that they are almost to the kayak launch on the other side of the river. I look outside my window and see a forecast sky full of pale white and gray weeping rain on a soaked landscape.

Me:"Its fucking raining..."

William: "Maybe up by you but the weather down here is sunny with scattered showers." "Are you still coming?"

Me: "If the weather is holding out by you guys, then I don't see why not." I hang up and grab my overnight camping bag. I march down into the drive and hitch my kayak to the roof of my Subaru Forester. During the process, an errant bungee hook snapped and kissed my windshield, leaving an ugly crack on the driver's side. If that wasn't an omen for what I was about to get myself into then maybe what followed was.

The drive from my house in Platte Clove on the mountain top into the Hudson lowlands near Port Ewen takes about an hour. I attempted to get breakfast for everyone as penance for running late at Bagel World in Kingston. The bagels however tasted like the boiled lips of a Rottweiler and soon caused me malaise as I parked my car at the Esopus Meadows preserve.

I stepped out into the pouring rain and disengaged my kayak and got her down to the water amongst an aquatic bramble of cruciferous looking plants. I thought this kid said it wasent fucking raining.

I pull out my phone.

William: "Hey man, we're already at the island and setting up our hammocks, where are you?"

Me:"I'm across the river from you guys in the town of Esopus." "I was about to set out but this weather is shit." "Maybe I should wait some"

William: "It's really not that bad once you get here man, I'm telling ya."

Me: "Uhhhhh,ok." I say skeptically as I look out at a drenched view that no longer resembles anywhere on Earth.

William: "I plan on performing a purification ritual to cleanse Crowley's influence from the island, but I would prefer to do this during daylight hours so try to get here soon." "I want you to bear witness."

Me: "Purification ritual?" "What?" "You mean like an exorcism?" "You're going to exercise the whole island?"

William: "Sort of, I can explain in greater detail once you are here." "How much longer?"

Me:" That will depend on the current and the weather." William: "Good luck!" "Let us know when you are close!" Red button.

I grab my pack and take my kayak out onto the Hudson with Ulster County on my stern, Hyde
Park off my bow, and my island destination starboard.

*　*　*

As I CUT THROUGH THE MURKY waters of America's Rhine towards the middle of the river, I feel a vibration in my pack, followed by the theme for Stranger Things. Ames is calling me from her job.

I pick up. Me:"Hello?"

Ames:"Hey, you're not still going on that kayak trip to that weird guy's island down south or whatever, right?"

Me:"Yeah, I'm already out on the water." "Just wish it would stop fucking raining."

Ames: "JESSE, YOU NEED TO GET TO LAND RIGHT NOW, THERE IS A THUNDERSTORM ADVISORY HEADING RIGHT FOR YOU, IF ITS NOT THERE ALREADY!"

ME: "WHAT!?"

Ames: "Jesse go to shore!" "Lightning tends to strike tall things and out on the water... I'm guessing that is you."

My anxiety sets in with a familiar punch in my chest followed by imaginary sweat trickling down my flushed, burning face. My equilibrium shuts off and destroys my balance. It feels like there is a fan blowing fire behind my ribs that causes my focus to float away from me like a helium balloon. Tears glaze my eyesight and cause a suddenly frightening world to distort as my breathing reaches a staccato. Next come the tremors that cause me to roll, pitch and yaw while my sanity bursts apart like a firework in 8 different directions at astonishing speed, begging me to chase but impossible to pursue.

I'm having a panic attack.

I become recumbent in the kayak for a moment while I begin to practice the coping mechanisms Ames has taught me to utilize at times like this. First thing I do is start burping. I know it sounds crazy but it works as a form of hyperventilation and serves as a breathing exercise to take back control of your body. Next thing I need is my mind. This part requires compartmentalization. Let's see if we can't wrangle those runaway fragments of my psyche. I need to find land, and I need to find it now. They say that you feel the hairs on your body prick up and a feeling like an electrical charge courses it way up through you nanoseconds before lightning strikes your body. Unless I want to experience that, I need to find somewhere to dock. That's the mission. That's what's more important than losing my shit right now. That's where my focus and all those errant thoughts need to go.

I can start to hear Ames yelling for me over the phone. I'm coming back.

Ames: "Je...........Jese......esse....."

I look over the port bow, and see the Esopus Lighthouse towering up out of the drink 0.2 miles away from where I'm drifting. I think I can make it.

I hold the phone back up to my face. Me: "LIGHTHOUSE!"

Ames: "WHAT!?"

Call ended.

I start paddling as hard as I can. If I can get to the Esopus lighthouse and wait out the storm then I promise myself a proper mental breakdown once I get there. Hell, I'll even spring for a phone call for help and give up on this gauche plan altogether. Canceling plans is like heroin.

My mind wanders to a giant mural painted alongside the brick wall in the alleyway outside The Chance music venue in Poughkeepsie, depicting a vicious sea serpent that legend claims was hundreds of feet long named "Kipsy, The Hudson River Monster." I remember reading about the various sightings and encounters of the beast throughout the river's history going all the way up to 2009. This is what anxiety does. These are the things it intrudes into your mind with. Nevertheless, the extra fear and thalassophobia that there might be a leviathan beneath me, dwarfing my small craft with its unfathomable size powers me at full steam to the aged and eroded stone steps that granted access to the lighthouse proper.

I tie my boat amidst kicking waves to the dock and fall upon the ground and without histrionics I tell you that I started kissing the rocky spire I was now unknowingly stranded upon.

At the top of the spiral stairway is a white picket fence brandishing a metal road sign warning me that I am currently on camera and entering without appointment from the Ulster County Historical Society will constitute trespassing.

Ok.

I push the swinging gate of the fence open and rush through a downpour to the lighthouse entrance.

Locked.

Well of course it is.

I turn and press my back against the door and slowly slump to the ground.

The pounding rain and screaming squalls churning the river waves all around me into angry foam are now finally joined by the thunderstorm that was promised which signals its arrival to the party with the invasive low frequency drum of a jet engine during takeoff. Lightning flashes across the sky of the Hudson Valley like a screenshot on a phone, and in the distance I can barely make out over two miles of turbulent waters, the dark island I was meant to be on right now.

ME: "HOW THE FUCK IS HE GONNA STAND THERE AND TELL ME THAT IT IS NOT RAINING BY HIM!?"

I pull my phone out like a gun and call William.

William: "Heyyyyyyyyyyyyyyyy, you getting close now buddy?"

Me: "NO, NO I AM NOT CLOSE" "I AM NOWHERE NEAR CLOSE AS A MATTER OF FACT."

"I AM PINNED DOWN AT THE MOMENT BY THE ELEMENTS AT A FUCKING LIGHTHOUSE TWO MILES NORTH OF YOUR POSITION!" "WHICH OUT ON THE OPEN WATER....IS A FUCKING LONG ASS WAY!" "WILLIAM....YOU SAID YOU GUYS WERE EXPERIENCING SCATTERED SHOWERS, NOT THE PERFECT FUCKING STORM."

William: "Hey, I'm gonna need you to calm down man." "Just relax" I just checked Hudson Valley weather.com earlier when the rain started to pick up and it says this is all supposed to pass in like a half hour." "Are you alright?"

Me: "Not really man, I am in the thrall of a serious panic attack and I can't get inside the lighthouse for shelter cause some colonial cosplaying geezers locked the fucking door!" "I'm getting soaked and it's freezing out here." "And on top of all that my phone battery is almost dea......"

"........."

William: "...Jesse?"

I see it.

My bright red kayak aimlessly tossing about the western shore of the lighthouse to the dance of the surrounding tempest, the half hitch knot I had tied it to the dock with is trawling uselessly behind it.

Me: "NO!"

The storm must have bucked her loose like some goddamn nautical rodeo. I drop my phone into a garden box beside the lighthouse main entrance as William yells reassuringly beyond my attention that once the storm passes he will come find me.

I push past the swinging gate again and dive off the stairs into the violent black depths, not giving a tinker's damn about the chop above or the bull sharks below.

Oh yes, bull sharks that came as far up the freshwater Hudson as Athens, NY for feeding and breeding this time of year, were so called bull sharks because of their highly aggressive nature. They famously patrol shorelines when hunting and for all I knew were circling me below, waiting to tear me apart like a cherry pie thrown out onto an active dance floor.

"Jesse "James" Angelino killed by sharks on his way to an exorcism" is what the pape's will read.

"We all saw this coming..." my buddy Nat would address the grieving at my wake with.

If that kayak gets away with my phone on low battery then who knows how long I might be stranded on this rock.

The current here is unbelievably strong but I don't have far to go. Once I am able to grab a hold of the kayak, its buoyancy is able to give me an assist back to the miniature bank of the lighthouse and eventually return me to the dock. This time I pull the kayak onto shore with me and drag it up the stairs like a furious waterlogged ghoul.

Me: "OH NO YOU FUCKING DONT!" "THIS IS NOT THE HILL I AM WILLING TO FUCKING DIE ON OUT HERE!" "DO YOU UNDERSTAND ME!?" I shout at my vessel.

The kayak sits beached and unresponsive amidst a margin of earth and brush.

The storm around me couldn't possibly soak me any more as I was. My energy and morale dipping, I once more ascended the stairs and pushed through the swinging gate in order to get to the garden box where I had let my phone fall.

I fish my phone out of the garden box's bush and use my fingers to smudge away the condensation on the tiny screen to reveal layered text messages from William.

He says that the storm had passed at the island and he was taking his raft out to come find me. He assures me that if I just remain where I am, help is on its way…

I message him back that I will remain where I am until he arrives but my phone instead tells him that "I am made of rye bread."

Auto correct will be the death of poetry, mark my words.

I try to huddle as close as I can beneath the awning above the lighthouse door to avoid the rain and disassociate into reverie until William can find me.

Hours go by before I take my phone out from where it had been drying in my pack to see that I have a missed call from William's wife Airy. I hit her back up.

Me: "Please tell me something nice…"

Airy: "Jesse, has William reached you by now?" "He left hours ago to come find you but he forgot his phone here and doesn't have any water with him and I am starting to worry."

Me: "That's like…the opposite of what I asked."

Airy: "Jesse, I'm serious!" "He said you were only two miles away, can't you at least see him!?"

I turn towards the gulf that separates my 34 foot spit of land from their island and see nothing but the weather finally breaking.

Me: "Airy, I cannot see him" "He did know to go north right?" "Not south?" Airy begins to sob and cry on the phone.

Airy: "I don't know, he was really worried about you in the storm and rushed out to find you without any prep whatsoever." "It all happened so fast!" "He just jumped into the raft and took off and now I'M freaking out because you weren't picking up and I have no way of reaching him!"

I try to calm her down but as drained as I am, it's like trying to thread a sausage through a needle.

Now William is missing out on the water and I have to do something. My battery is at 14%. It's now or never.

I dial 911.

There is a special place in hell for people who call the cops on themselves, right next to guys who order their hamburgers rare at a restaurant for masculinity's sake. Is there any more abhorrent behavior that exudes more "My wife wont fuck me anymore" energy than that?

Emergency Dispatch: "911, what is your emergency?"

Me: "My name is Jesse Angelino and I am currently stranded at the Esopus lighthouse out on the Hudson river.

I risk more of my phone's battery to check my phone's compass app.

"I am at latitude 41.8684 degrees north, latitude 73. 9416 west in between Ulster and Dutchess counties!" "A friend of mine attempted to ride out to meet me but has been missing out on the water for over an hour now." "Please send help!"

Emergency Dispatch: "Alright Jesse, we have a police boat with scuba recovery and rescue inbound to your position from Albany." ``Just sit tight and we will be there soon, are you hurt at all?"

Me: 'DID YOU SAY ALBANY!?" " WHAT THE FUCK!?" "THAT'S OVER 60 MILES AWAY!?" "DON'T YOU HAVE ANYTHING CLOSER!?"

Emergency dispatch: "SIR." "UNLESS YOU ARE INJURED OR UNLESS THIS IS AN ACTUAL EMERGENCY THAN THAT IS THE CLOSEST BOAT WE ARE ASSIGNING TO COME AND GET YOU."

I dont have the strength to fight this woman. Red Button.

Another hour goes by. Then another. It's almost 5. The sun is getting low.

I can see something traveling against the current up the eastern shoreline that I departed from.

The rising heat makes it impossible to clearly identify through the refraction coming off the water but it looks like a speck moving towards me.

In another forty minutes the speck on the horizon morphs into William on his raft powering upriver towards my marooned ass! He is a tonic for tired eyes, miserable as he seemed, a soaked scarecrow marinating in sweat and PCB battling his way to my finite shoreline with a stick. I rush down the steps to the dock and pull him from the raft onto shore as soon as he is close enough. He collapses in a heap and turns to me barely with breath.

William: "if.....you...weren't....here....after...all...that...we...weren't.... going.....to be....friends...anymore..."

He looks past me toward the towering lighthouse. William: "What is this?"

I help him to his feet.

Me: "WELCOME TO THE MAID OF THE MEADOWS YOUNG RESCUER."

* * *

ANOTHER HOUR GOES BY at the lighthouse where myself and William become living allegories for Robert Pattinson and Willem Dafoe's roles in the actual motion picture "The Lighthouse" as we both spiral into madness due to the mounting circumstances we have found ourselves in. William wants me to ride with him in the raft back to the island but I am too afraid of going back into the water and it was paving the way for some rough conversation. I gave him the awful food from

Bagel World that I bought earlier which he does not seem to mind. What a ringing endorsement.. "Bagel World, you won't even have time to realize that our sandwiches taste like animal cloaca if you're in a life or death situation."

William: "Well, we can't stay here, my wife is probably worried sick over there, and if what you're telling me is true and the police are on their way then I need to get word to Airy." "We have uh....some mind altering substances at our camp for the purification ritual that I would rather not chance them finding should they come sniffing around."

Me: "What if I have another panic attack while I'm out on the water?" "I don't want to go through that again."

William: "It's ok, I'll be here to talk you down this time." "My raft is much bigger than the kayak so you don't have to feel claustrophobic riding in it with me." "We'll just tow the kayak behind us and bounce before the law gets here."

I agree and before long, we are out on open water once more, bee lining towards that evil sorcerer's island, this time with the sun shining down on us and the weather dryer than a chameleon's clavicle. We almost lost my kayak two minutes into our departure after its rudder groove was snagged by underwater vines from some invasive water chestnuts, but William plunged his arms into the deep and managed to free them.

About 25 minutes into us rowing with the current I begin to hear a motor from behind us. I turn and see a police boat completely blowing past the lighthouse and now bearing down on us.

Me: "William!" "It's the cops!""They finally came!" William turns to see them.

William: "Row faster!"

Me: "What!?" "Are you out of your fucking mind!?" "We can't outrun that!!"

The patrol boat catches up to us in moments, veering up on our portside and cutting the engine to hail us, while William jokingly shouts that we are being boarded. The first officer we see looks like he does not have a single shred of patience to spare. He is sunburnt all across his arms and face and is wearing some cool looking aquatic uniform with a Kraken wrapping its tentacles around the inscription "Ulster County Sheriff In-water Rescue Unit" where his badge should be. We can also see another officer pushing the boat wheel hardover to cut us off in the water as if we could somehow escape at this point. He wears the same uniform but with a 9 mm strapped to his hip.

Officer 1: "One of you boys called dispatch cause you were trapped by that storm earlier?"

Me:`That would be me, officer." "I was pinned down by the weather at the Esopus Lighthouse for most of the day, and was worried I wouldn't make it off that rock til my friend here showed up and got me."

I gesture to William who waves.

William:"Now that the weather cleared up, we can make it the rest of the way by ourselves, thanks!!"

The officer removes his Ray Ban WayFarers and looks at us with an intensity that borders on madness. I had seen more life in an animal's eyes.

Officer: "Oh you boys are coming with us." "We just came all the way down from the goddamn capital, now we're taking you back to shore!" 'You boys aren't wearing life jackets, which is against maritime law."

Honestly I have been kayaking for over 15 years and had no idea that that was true.

The officer: ``I should be issuing you both tickets right about now, but on account we took so long to get here I'ma let you boys off with just a warning!"

Officer 2: "Please proceed onboard and my partner here will see to your crafts!"

We did as we were told and crawled out off the raft and onto the patrol boat and as promised, the first officer dragged our raft and kayak onto the back deck.

William: "Officer please, my wife is expecting us at that island over there!" He points to Crowley's Island.

William: "I know you gotta take us to shore but maybe you could take us to the island instead?" "It's technically a shore." "And I just know that she's terrified for my safety right about now!"

The two officers look at each other and exchange a huge smile.

Officer 1: "Bet she's madder than a wet hen at ya for going out in that storm like that, huh?" It seems to amuse them to no end that Airy's response to us being dropped off at the island by police was tantamount to a death sentence.

Officer 2: "Bet she'll give ya a good hollerin if we were to take you guys on out there,eh?" What the fuck is wrong with these guys.

William: "Yes!" "She will be very upset, there will be loads of yelling!" William nudges me to go along with this because it's making them less hostile to us.

Me: "Yea, she might even belt us in the mouth as soon as she sees us!"

William looks at me like I took it too far, but the two officers look like Christmas morning.

Officer 2: "Hot damn, we'll bring you boys to the missus alright." "Just make sure you put these to good use tomorrow when you lot head back out on the water!"

He reaches into a metal container full of life jackets that match the ones he and his partner are wearing and assigns us 3. (They look really awesome and I still have mine to this day.)

The patrol boat makes a short journey across the two miles that separated us from Crowley's shores but the officers filled the awkward silence by asking what sort of cruel and damning things William's wife was going to do to us once they dropped us off, practically licking their chops and ringing their hands like Dr. Frankenstein, the fucking weirdos.

As soon as the patrol boat enters the bay of the island and prepares to land we can already see Airy standing with her arms crossed, ready to slap the both of us harder than a drunk southern widow, drawn to the inlet by the boat's loud motor interrupting the island's dark peace. Body language that was easily read by the two officers who were reveling in this sadism by hooting and loudly announcing how fucked the two of us were. Once we are close enough, they allow us to disembark and drag our boats to the island's beach while they proceed to whistle and cat call out to Airy in her bathing suit.

Officer 2: "You sure you don't want to come with us honey!?" "Leave these two fellas here?"

* * *

ONCE THE POLICE LEAVE, Airy leads us up to the campsite where she has already hidden whatever it was William was so concerned the police might find earlier after observing the entire ordeal from the high vantage point that the island's north shore offered. Once our safety was confirmed she became angry with William and started chastising him for his reckless behavior. I was so exhausted by everything that had happened that I decided to take a stroll to the island's south shore until cooler heads prevailed. As I followed the marked trail through skeleton trees and wet crags of stone I could feel my anxiety returning and a panic attack imminent. I stopped and stared at a cluster of pale writhing wormlike creatures that were crawling all over each other in a disgusting heap on top of the wave stricken rocks in the surf. Whatever they were, the very sight of them all amassed like that sent me into revulsion. I had made it off the Lighthouse sure, but now I was once again stranded in this evil place without the option of leaving for fear of what might become of me out on the water should I try to go it alone. William and Airy were now also under the diabolical thrall that this place seemed teeming with and as I caught the fear, these two continued to battle it out with increasing aggression.

This place is cursed.

After everything I just wanted to be far from here with Ames. I wanted to go home.

I returned to the campsite and saw that the fighting was over for now. William had retired to his hammock for a nap and Airy was passive aggressively collecting firewood. I approached her and told her that I needed to leave this place or I was going to lose my mind. That I needed to get to Ames.

Being far from anything familiar in the company of wrath and trepidation on an island infamous for its malevolent past was not doing my apprehensive brain any favors in this instance.

Airy: "Well, William just passed out and he's probably shot after going to look for you, and I really don't want to take the raft out by myself so do you think you can just hang out until he wakes up and I'll see if he can bring you back to the closer shoreline." It's only a 20 minute paddle to the mainland from this side of the river but I just don't want to chance anything else going wrong today."

Me: "I'm sorry Airy but I cannot wait for William to wake up, my panic attacks have been absolutely vicious as of late." "If I stay in these doldrums any longer I am too afraid of what might happen." "By the way,

I saw what looked like living rattlesnake eggs squirming around on the south shore, so…you know…look out for that."

I turn and use what's left of my dying phone battery to contact 911 dispatch once again, patching me through to the boat that had literally just rescued us, and requesting an extraction from this iniquitous sandbar.

They shout at me and tell me that they "aren't a taxi" at first, but eventually agree to come back one last time to scoop me and my kayak and bring me to the marina in Staatsburg where they have an ambulance waiting to check me out since they were concerned over my hysterics on the phone. Once I was on real land again, the first responders told me that I was dangerously dehydrated from all the rowing, crying, sweating and exercise that I had done over the course of the day, and that these psychological fits I kept having were my body's way of getting my attention. (So it ended up being a really good thing that I didn't end up staying.)

They contact Ames to come pick me up and stay with me while I wait making sure to give me plenty of water. As for Ames, there but for the grace of God goes she who left work early to recover me from such a disaster.

Now do I believe that old master of darkness had my mission damned since jump street?

Not exactly, but for a guy who allegedly used black magick to bind his own guardian angel in order to move beyond God's sight and therefore his love, would it be any wonder?

5

The Depraved Gambit's Of the Acheampong Twins

I HAVE TRIED MY VERY BEST so far, to truly describe the eclectic row of people that I choose to surround myself with and deliver to you, the reader, their colorful and wide-ranging personalities here on paper. But I tell you now dear readers that there will nary be a rarer breed like the Acheampong twins, Aliyah and Micah. The hilarious and hebraic, ebony transfer students from West Africa.

Myself, Aliyah and Micah met while attending grade school. Aliyah sat behind me and would whisper quotes from Jon Lovitz's beloved comedy cartoon "The Critic" in my ear, which would cause me to erupt with laughter that would often get me scolded by the teacher and let's be honest, make me look like a fucking idiot in class.

As for Micah, I remember his own personal brand of hellish hyjinx starting early in life when he managed to burgle our teacher's Ram-Man action figure from the Masters Of The Universe franchise. I don't know how he did it, but he managed to smuggle it past a backpack to backpack search conducted at the end of the day in order to discover the culprit.

As Aliyah, her brother and I grew older, Dunkaroos and Saturday morning cartoons on FOX made way for late night sessions of smoking weed in Aliyah's first car and drinking Japanese sake out in the graveyard.

Micah was adept at matching exciting situations to otherwise common coming of age tropes involving experiments with weed and alcohol. He would tell all of us when we were smoking in his sister's car late at night that any given passing pair of headlights could potentially "spot us" and demand we duck every time they drove by. (Even though we were parked in their driveway.) My first few times getting high would predictably make me feel strange and act even stranger. I would yell about a mistaken belief I harbored where I could manipulate electricity and tried to mimic the hissing sounds that bolts of lightning being generated from my body would make to accompany such a phenomenon.

Aliyah would assist this foolish sight by turning the radio up and down and flashing the interior dome lights from her driver's seat yelling "HE'S DOING IT!"

After such guerilla theater had concluded, Aliyah would use my phone to prank call a local strip club, using her most sensuous voice to pose as various women seeking auditions for a job, each more ludicrous than the last.

Strip club proprietor: "Gentlemen's club, how can I help you?"

Aliyah: "Hi, my name is Alyssa Sutton and I was wondering if I could come in this saturday and try out my routine for the owner?" "Ya know, see if I can get a permanent gig over there?"

SCP: "Uhhhhhh, routine?"

Donnie: "Yea, it's called "Restricted for your own safety". "See what i do is, I come out with my hair all messed up, real 80's hair metal like, wearing a straight jacket made of caution tape that boys can unwrap off of me, ya know like it's christmas."

SCP: "......uh."

Aliyah: "And as soon as the whole thing is off, I leap on their tables and scream in their face!" "AHHHHHHHHHHHHH" "HYUGAHHHH-HHHHHHH!"

SCP: "…….YOUR THAT FUCKING GIRL FROM LAST WEEK WHO KEPT CALLING IN AND COMPLAINING THAT EVERYONE WAS ONLY TIPPING HER WITH MAGIC THE GATHERING CARDS HERE!!!!"

Explosions of laughter.

I could write a whole book off of just the twins' exploits alone but for the sake of time I am going to narrow it down to a chapter I look back on as "the longest day of my life". A holiday tale about how you can "dress em up, but you sure as shit cant take em out."

* * *

IT WAS DECEMBER AND CHRISTMAS was fast approaching, when one of our lady friends, Selena, had told us all about a holiday party her grandfather was letting her throw at her job for the staff and loyal patrons of a restaurant where she waitressed at. Selena was a well liked, very pretty, friendly, and ambitious girl from our class who tried to include as many people as possible whenever she hosted festivities. Though her own immediate social circle operated much like a college sorority and kept up appearances like carrying tiny dogs in their purses, drinking commercially available latte's all day and bragging about their bras, which would cost in excess of $200 while strutting through the school halls in pumps, she was admittedly not as stuck up or as airheaded as people often suspected her to be and she treated everyone at school with kindness and respect. Her grandfather was the owner of the restaurant and employed one of our other friends, Tony, there as kitchen help. She invited myself and Aliyah to stop by and enjoy the free food and open bar if we could make it. There was always a thrilling and tolerable danger when drinking at a bar underage so we were in.

* * *

Part 1, The Morning Of (Jesse, 7AM)

THE DAY STARTED OUT at my then girlfriend's house, Stacey. Stacey was an adorable art student with a very disarming personality. She dyed her hair different colors monthly, worked on sculptors and paintings, would nullify her own anxieties by reading children's books to herself, and was constantly dreaming up strange and unique clothing styles that she would then will into existence with needle and thread. Every once in a while I would sneak into her house and spend the night with her, carefully avoiding her mother who hated me. That morning, she had woken up before me to catch the bus to school, and had assured me that her mother had left for work already but that her brother was staying home. I would have to figure out how to exit the house without him spotting me. This also meant I was not going to be able to take the bus into school with her. I opted to sleep on it.

When I woke up an hour later, It had dawned on me that I had better start using what time was left to me and split before I was caught, as Stacey's mom was known to stop home randomly throughout the day and her brother Anthony was still in the house. I crept over to Stacey's door and cracked it so as to listen for any movement. If he was in his room I could just bolt for the front door before he discovered me. Maybe I would get lucky and he would be taking a really long shit.. As I pointed my ear toward the opening I could hear the tv in his room playing Yu-gi-oh at max volume. But then...he also had The Matrix movie going at full audio on the living room tv as well, and the same deal with Law & Order SVU in their mothers room! "FUCK!" I hissed. "Who the hell does this?" "He could be anywhere in the fucking house right now!"

I tried to think. There were three different televisions in three different parts of the house which meant I could not determine exactly where he was and because he had chosen for some reason to have them all running at their loudest volume I could not pinpoint any footsteps, throat clearing, toilets flushing, NADA, to determine his immediate position.

I closed the door and looked around the room in panic. Stacey had a window above her bed, but it was a narrow slit that I really didn't think that I was going through.But there was no way else. If Anthony caught me and told his mom, then the jig would be up and I could kiss my overnight stays here goodbye. I jumped up on her bed and immediately started turning the crank to open the window. Once it was agape, I managed to easily toss my overnight bag out through it and down into the alleyway below.

All right. Here goes.

I pull myself up to the slitted window and start compressing my torso like a rat to fit through. It's actually working to some extent, but it is an arduous process of sucking in my stomach and worming gently through the portal.

Aha!

I am able to get my upper torso through! Now to just wiggle my hips and legs out and everything will be just...

Without warning, Stacey's room is filled with the ungodly tocsin of an alarm going off . Its 9:00 on the dot and her Hello Kitty clock, set to go off at this time for no other reason I can think of but to fuck me right now, is sounding off an unpleasent series of repetitious whines that could wake the dead.

My heart stops and my eyes roll around in my head like Stevie Wonder. Im fucked. The alarm is louder than all three of the televisions cranked up volumes. Anthony is definitely going to hear this and come investigate. He will be here in seconds, and I can't writhe back inside before he storms in and finds me like this. What the fuck do I do!? I keep trying to hoist myself the rest of the way through frantically but I am not so lythe as to be able to get my butt through in time.

Stacey's door bursts open. I can't see him, but I know Anthony is there. I can hear his signature stomping like a fever stricken madman entering the room and approaching me in my Winnie The Pooh dilemma. I stop struggling and give up. The die has been cast.

I listen as he shuts off the alarm clock and then....nothing. What is happening?

I straighten myself out so as to look back inside expecting to see Anthony staring back at me. But he's already gone.

Even closed the door behind him on his way out. I'm speechless.

No way.

"Anthony!" I whisper loudly back into the room, thinking it impossible he could have missed me.

How could he?

How do you miss a pair of human legs in black skinny jeans hanging out of the only window in the room, against a completely white wall, 8 inches away from the very alarm you just turned off? He was close enough for me to have kicked if I'd had a mind to at that moment. But as I stare in disbelief for a few minutes, waiting for Anthony's return I am eventually forced to accept the Christmas miracle that I was just a part of. Sleepy son of a bitch must have been too tired to see me!

Without further delay I start heaving the rest of my body out the window and eventually fall out of the other side. I drop down into the alley and quickly grab my pack and start walking casually towards the road, pulling out my cell phone and turning it on so I can call one of my partners-in-crime, Aliyah.

She picks up.

Aliyah: "Good morning 007, congratulations on getting out of that pickle." "I'm on my way to you in 5!"

* * *

Part 2, The morning of (Aliyah, 7AM)

DURING MY TIME TRYING to make good my escape from Stacey's house, Aliyah and her sister-in-law, Callie,(Who was also Micah's wife.) were in the breakfast line at the Mcdonalds on the opposite side of town.

Mcdonalds Employee: "Hello!" "Welcome to Mcdonalds, can I help you?" Aliyah: "Yeah, you guys accepting any applications?"

Mcdonalds Employee: "No, I am sorry." "Our staff is currently at capacity." Aliyah whispers to Callie.

Aliyah: "Curious, isn't it?" "6 minutes they've kept us waiting, but their staff is at capacity?" "Fast food they dare call it..."

Callie: "Aliyah, don't be rude."

Mcdonalds employee: "...are you guys not ready to order?" Callie: "Let's see, I'll have...a...."

Aliyah: "Callie, you've had six minutes, its Mcdonalds, the menu hasn't changed in like 30 fucking years, it's the same six things,whats the hold up?" "You should already know what you want when you're walking in ''.

Callie: "You're the one who invited me out Aliyah!" "Don't rush me!" They get their food and go.

Back in Aliyah's Nissan Altima, over a couple of breakfast sandwiches, Callie is informed of the reason her sister-in-law has summoned her out so early.

Callie: "You want me to punch you in the eye!?" Aliyah: "Yes..."

Callie: "What the fuck, NO!" "I'M NOT DOING THAT!" Aliyah: "Callie, please..."

Callie: "WHAT THE FUCK FOR!?"

Aliyah: "I need you to give me a black eye so I can call out of work and go to Selena's party later." "I'm going to convince my boss that I was jumped by some rando's last night and that I can't make it in today, but if I'm going to really sell this Callie, I'm gonna need a good shiner."

Callie: "So you called me out for breakfast, hoping that I would punch you in the eye, and give you a bruise that you can exploit to get out of work?"

Aliyah: "Yes, I and I need that pretty soon cause I gotta call this lady ASAP." Callie: "I...I don't really know about this"

Aliyah: "Callie...I'm asking you as my twin brother's wife." "Please punch me in my fucking face so i dont have to go to work today."

Callie: "Fine" "You paid for breakfast, I'll punch you in your face if that's what you really want."

* * *

AFTER BREAKFAST THEY CRUISE back to Aliyah's place. Callie is still lackluster about hitting Aliyah in the face until she is able to recall a past incident during her first time at Aliyah's and her husband's parents house for Thanksgiving dinner, where she looked the fool after Aliyah convinced her it was her family's tradition to dress as historically appropriate pilgrims to the event. The surprised look on everyone's face when she arrived wearing a smock, petticoat, bodice, stockings, latchet shoes and even a bonnet while everyone sat in plain clothes and Aliyah cackled at the head of the dinner table, serves as a brilliant catalyst with which Callie then uses to deliver the promised southpaw into Aliyah's right side orbital socket as hard as she can, which blossoms into the desired bruise after only a half hour.

Aliyah: "Thanks Callie, you're the best!"

Callie: "I gotta get to my law class...say hi to Jesse for me, oh and don't forget to pick up your brother on the way." "Selena invited us to the event as well but I got too much studying tonight." "Good luck."

Callie exits the apartment as Aliyah's phone starts to ring. It's our friend Tony I mentioned earlier.

Tony was always a bit of a loner, who preferred death metal and solitude,hanging upside down off his home gym while reading medical journals concerning morbid anatomy, to socializing with most of us, but he was not a bad guy by any stretch of the imagination. Just different.

Aliyah: "Hello"

Tony: "Hey!" "How's it going!?"

Aliyah: "Callie just punched me in the face." Tony: " what!?"

Aliyah: "What's going on with you?"

Tony: "Uhhhh, I was wondering if you had heard from Jesse at all?" "I want to make sure he's still coming to the holiday party tonight, but I just ran into Stacey in the hallway and she told me that she's worried he's trapped at her house and cant get out."

Aliyah: "He slept over again without her mom knowing, huh?" Tony: "Seems to be the case."

Just then, Aliyah see's my call coming in.

Aliyah; "Speak of the devil and he will appear, gotta go Tony!"

Tony: "Call me back!" She switches calls.

Aliyah: "Good morning 007, congratulations on getting out of that pickle!" "I'm on my way to you in 5!"

* * *

Part 3, The afternoon of (Me and Aliyah, 12PM)

ALIAYAH: "HALF OF THE ADVERTISEMENTS on daytime radio are for sports betting and the other half is for gambling addiction hotlines.' "God damn it Jesse, I cant wait for this fucking crumbling empire to finally die."

She says this while adjusting the tuner in her car. Me: "What happened to your eye?"

Aliyah: "Like it?" "It's so I could tell my boss I got marred in a fight last night and can't go

to work, why didn't you go to class?

Me: 'I couldn't leave Stacey's to catch the bus because I think her brother is going deaf...and blind too for that matter."

* * *

ALIYAH PULLS INTO MY HOME DRIVEWAY. The house I grew up in is huge and has three bathrooms, so we can both get ready for the party at the same time later. The first thing we both notice when we enter my house through the kitchen is my sister Layla's boyfriend, Arthur, sitting at the island in the center of the room and flipping through one of my old weekly planners that I used the previous summer while interning in Manhattan for my dad's brother at MTV. (Smart phone's weren't a thing yet and you still had to write appointments down if you didn't want to forget about them.) I must have forgotten about it after school started up again and left it lying around.

Arthur stares down at one of the pages he holds open fervently, then looks at me from under a camo hat advertising beer with stern concern.

Arthur: "Jesse, you do some weird shit man..." "I just don't know about you sometimes"

Myself: "What are you talking about?" "What in that book do you find "weird, Arthur?"

Arthur holds the planner up and displays a date from last August on a Sunday where I scheduled myself to meet with my sister for lunch at a local restaurant in our area called "Bread Alone", while visiting from the city one weekend.

Arthur: "You dont think this is weird?" "That you wrote down and planned to eat bread BY YOURSELF!?"

Me: "Arthur, god damn it….the restaurant is called "BREAD ALONE", What did you think?" "That I was going solo on some King's Hawaiian?"

I snatch the planner and keep it moving towards the stairs with Aliyah behind me shaking her head at Arthur.

Aliyah: "See?" "You see?" "That boy right there is why ya'll never see any black serial killers"

"Just white boys, goin through your things, thinkin all kinds of dumb shit and trying to get smacked!" "I swear, one day they're gonna be going through our phones too!" "Mark my words!"

* * *

Part 4, The night of (Myself, Aliyah, Micah,Tony and Selena, 7PM)

WE PICK UP MICAH EN ROUTE to the restaurant just as a nor'easter sets in across the Hudson Valley.

The scene is a jovial one inside the old log cabin style cafe, bedecked with yuletide decor, a serve yourself buffet with steam table pans offering up roast beef, lemon chicken, garlic mashed potatoes, sweet corn,line caught salmon, and the like all laid out across from the bar where Selena is serving drinks to a throng of loyal patrons and house staff.

Aliyah, Micah and I order some whiskey sours and move about the room getting to know the regulars here. Aliyah, who is a former member of the United States Coast Guard, finds herself pleasantly locked in conversation with a retired Marine named Jerry, who sits at the end of the bar with his glass of brown and ice explaining to the merry gathering that a true bourbon has to be made with at least 51% corn and must also be from America, whereas true whiskey must only be made with grain.

This interesting tidbit causes Aliyah to switch from the jejune whiskey sour to the NEWFOUND complexity of the bourbon cocktails Selena is making.

A trade off that would affect her constitution for the worse.. Jerry: "So what branch did you say you served in again?" Aliyah: "Coast Guard sir!"

Jerry: "Oh yeah?" "Where'd they station you?"

Aliyah: "Cleveland, actually."

Jerry nearly spits out his drink.. Jerry:" you mean Ohio!?"

Aliyah: "Yeah, that's where Cleveland is." Jerry: "Its fucking land locked!"

Aliyah: "Not Lake Erie sir."

Jerry nearly falls off his barstool, red cheeked and howling with laughter in Aliyah's unamused face.

He then follows up this rude behavior with a mocking salute towards Aliyah who is chugging her drink to stay calm."

Jerry: "Well thank you SO MUCH for your bravery and service to this country ma'am!" 'HAHAHAHAHAHAHAHA"

Aliyah moves on to find better conversation elsewhere while Jerry continues to patronize her for protecting us from the "scary Canadians across the way."

She is not addressing anyone in particular at this point, just sort of talking at Salena and the people waiting for their drinks at the bar and doing her best to ignore the loud jeerings of the former Marine behind her.

Aliyah: "Ya know, earlier I was thinking to myself, what possible harm would it do to society if they just let Ted Kacyznski live out his last days in that cabin in the woods?"

"Then I remember…oh right, the bombs."

The head waitress Diana has noticed that Aliyah is starting to sway while mentioning all this.

Diana: "Hey Aliyah!"

Aliyah gives Diana an inappropriately intimate smile. Aliyah: "Hello vampire legs…"

Diana: "Why don't you slow down on those and help yourself to some food for a while, eh?" "Go make like some ants on a picnic and eat something."

Just then, Micah, who is now keeping pace with his twins drinking, makes the loud retort,

Micah: "Ants!" "Just think of how utterly unbelievable ants are by description!" "Oh, they live in complex societies underground?" "In your walls!?" "They eat your snacks and they have a queen!?" "They can lift 100 times their body weight!?" "Gaslight me some more!"

Diana walks over and gently takes Micah's whiskey sour.

Diana: "Alright you too, Time for a break." "Go eat." "Jesse, help them." I walk over to Aliyah.

Jesse: "Hey girl, we got lots of food here, wanna check it out?" Aliyah: "I have to go to the bathroom."

Me: "Alright, the restroom is right this way."

Micah follows us out to the back of the restaurant where the bathrooms are, and I tell Aliyah that I'll be back by the time she's done and return to the front. Micah starts walking towards the men's room and I return to the front of the house.

Almost 15 minutes go by and no one has heard or seen Aliyah or Micah since they both went to the little boys/girls room. I kept eying the hallway to catch either of them if they came out but had noticed nothing as of yet. Selena asks me to go find them as both of them are famously wanton for trouble after a few drinks, and clearly Jerry's antagonization had driven Aliyah to indulge more than usual.

By themselves, the two of them are mildly mischievous at best but together they are like those video game mini bosses that you have to defeat, and then face again a few levels later except now they are both glowing red and twice as hard.

I return to the men's room and push the door open. Micah is gone.

It was just then that I started to notice the sound of a toilet flushing over and over

again without reprieve next door in the woman's lavatory.

Shit, I never actually watched him come in here, I think to myself as I rush back out and into the women's room.

I burst through the door and immediately feel my feet get soaked.

I look down and see the entire floor flooded with 3-4 inches of water, all erupting from a toilet that Aliyah is wildly packing to the brim with scented potpourri chips that she tears violently from a decorative tray next to her.

I close the door and lock it in panic.

Me: "WHAT ARE YOU DOING ALIYAH!?"

Aliyah stops clogging the toilet and stumbles towards me, her feet treading water like we're on the sinking Titanic.

Aliyah:"Jesse, thank god you've arrived!" "We gotta get the fuck out of here!" "This place is a haven for nazi's!" "I think they invited me here as part of some sort of trap!"

Me: "Aliyah, I dont know what the fuck your talking about!" "You're drunk!" "Help me pull all this shit out!" "We have to get this cleaned up fast!"

I shoulder check past her in true high school hallway fashion towards the devastatingly clogged toilet, the shove causing an entire myriad of high end cutlery to fall out her jacket pockets.

I look down to where a Wustof butcher's cleaver falls to the submerged floor, followed by an 8 inch Misen Chef's knife, and then a cavalcade of sterling silverware.

Me: "Jesus, where the hell did you get all that!?" "WHAT THE FUCK IS GOING ON!?"

Aliyah: "Well Jesse if you must know, these are reparations I am taking back from those fucks for burning my ancestors alive in ovens 60 years ago!"

I come face to face with her now.

Me: "What are you saying!?" "We are in Selena's grandfather's restaurant in Catskill!"

"Where are you getting nazi's from!?" "Start making sense right now, because they are going to call the cops when they see what you've done here!!!!"

She stoops down to recover the fallen cutlery, but I angrily push her back before she can reach them.

Then I noticed it.

When I shoved her, her chest was bulky and hard. Like something large and plastic was concealed in front of her chest underneath the jacket.

I pointed at her, the two of us arguing over a pile of knives in a room that was still flooding. Our aggressive movements are creating significant splashes around us now.

Aliyah: "Exactly!" "Selenas Grandfather!" "When did she say her grandfather came over here from Germany!?" "In 1945!?" "Think about it Jesse, why do you think he took off and came over here and set up shop in a small quiet mountain town!?" "Because the Allies were hot on his heels!" "That's why!"

Me: "ALIYAH, WHAT THE FUCK DO YOU HAVE UNDER THAT JACKET!?"

Aliyah: "I'll admit I got a little lost on my way back from using the bathroom, but Jesse you're never going to believe this, I stumbled onto a secret room that Selena's grandfather has in the back, all decked out in swastika's as well as all manner of nazi party trimmings!" "Now I'm telling you this place is under the control of the SS and we need to leave immediately!"

Her eyes look past me towards the doomed toilet.

Aliyah: "And maybe disrupt these bastards operations while we're at it."

Me: "Do you hear yourself right now?" "Selena's grandfather was 7 years old in 1945 when his parents left Germany and came to New York, which means he couldn't have been a nazi YOU

FUCKING PSYCHO!"

Aliyah: "Hitler had a youth program!"

Me: "WHY!?" "ALIYAH, WHY WOULD AN OLD MAN ON THE RUN FROM THE ALLIES, OPEN A RESTAURANT, WHERE PEOPLE COME AND GO ALL DAY LONG, AND THEN INSTALL A "SECRET" ROOM FULL OF DAMNING EVIDENCE FOR ANYONE PATRONIZING THE PLACE TO FIND!?"

There is banging on the door now.

Diana: "Open up!" "What's going on in there!?" "There's water flooding out from under the door and into the hallway out here!" "Let us in NOW!"

Oh no.

Aliyah readies herself to burst out the door and make a run for it through the crowd assembling on the other side, while safely adjusting whatever it was she had hidden on her person.

Me: "Aliyah...what is under your jacket?"

Aliyah looks at me like the Cheshire Cat, slowly unzipping her jacket to reveal the statue of Baby Jesus that was the main feature of an ornate Nativity scene featured in the guest area of the restaurant.

Aliyah: "He was my king first Jes..." Me: "How did you get that!?"

Aliyah: "I had to move this big angel out of the way in order to even get to him, but I wasn't too worried." "What was he gonna do?" "Tell me "Be not afraid?"

The former Marine from earlier breaches the doorway and looks stunned by what he sees. Aliyah shoves her way past him into the hallway and tries to make a quick exit but the mob led by Diana, a seriously pissed off Selena, a bewildered Tony, and a hysterically laughing Micah have got her and they are not letting her go. Aliyah struggles amidst the shouting crowd trying desperately to protect the little savior in her jacket from the swarming hands trying to wrestle it from her, but Micah is closest, and manages to grab it from her first in what looks like the craziest game of football you have ever witnessed.

Micah: "I HAVE LED THE CRUSADE AGAINST BOOT AND KNIFE INTO THE GAS CHOKED HORIZON FOR DECADES, BEYOND THE SEETHING RIVERS OF BLOOD, UNDER MY OWN BANNER AND BY THE GLINTING OF MY LAST POLEARM; ALONE!!!!!"

He turns to run with the Jesus after yelling all of this, but the mob finally wrests the fake babe away from Micah, the ferocious struggle sending the statue sailing across the room and crashing into the buffet, effectively ending the party.

With an expression of shock I take flight out the front door. No amount of damage control can fix what's behind me now. My flushed burning face cools in the snowstorm outside as Micah and Aliyah catch up to me, a bloodthirsty mob at our waterlogged heels. We sprint to Aaliyah's car, the two of them laughing through the adrenaline rush we are now all experiencing. The three of us are moving so quickly and so clumsily that we are able to make it inside the vehicle and Aliyah even manages to start it up, with her and her brother up front and myself in the backseat. But the mob is not far, and they descend on the car like raging bees. Aliyah tries to press the button to lock all the car doors but accidentally lowers her driver's side electric window instead, giving Jerry the retired marine, the avenue he needs to plunge his arm through the now open window, and yolk Aliyah with an American soldier's grip.

Aliyah:"FUCK!" "MICAH, DO SOMETHING!"

I slam down on the correct button to lock all the doors before more can come through.

Micah, still laughing for some reason,but nonetheless coming to his sister's immediate aid, leans over and presses the button to raise the electric window back up with the drunk Jerry's arm still inside, effectively capturing it. As the window rises, it begins to crush his arm against its threshold , his blood flow becoming too restricted to maintain his grip on Aliyah and he is forced to release her.

Jerry: "MY FUCKING ARM!"

Aliyah: "You mean MY FUCKING ARM NOW SHITHEAD !"

Aliyah seizes this opportunity to throw her car in reverse and backs out of the crazed rabble, dragging the shrieking Jerry along for the ride, his arm still trapped inside and causing him to be thrashed about with the car's movements like a limp rag doll. His caterwauling of agony does not escape Aliyah's fragile attention and she lowers the window enough for the man so he can have his arm back, he falls to the ground, gripping it like a gunshot wound. She punches the gas and plows away from the screeching and wounded retiree, and out towards the main road, as the furious crowd behind us curses us with contempt and watches on as we speed off into the night, thus ending "The Longest day of my life."

6

The City That Never Sleeps (So why should I?)

IN THE SUMMER OF 2018, I was dating a girl from Oyster Bay, Long Island named Eliza. Aesthetically, she was an impressive young woman with dark features that cooperated with each other to the extent that she was considered by most to be a "smokeshow". She presented herself as one of those new age girls that wanted to climb the corporate ladder in some professional office job setting that paid lots of money but still did tarot readings and collected crystals behind the scenes. I didn't actually believe in any of that stuff, a testament to how guys like myself would humor almost anything to keep an arm charm like her. She would scream at me whenever I would return home from work at night, and plug my cell phone into its charger amidst the various precious stones she had accrued over the years on the table beside our bed for easy access.

Eliza: "YOU FUCKING IDIOT!" "DON'T YOU KNOW THAT THE RADIO FREQUENCIES THAT CELL PHONES GIVE OFF EMIT ELECTROMAGNETIC ENERGY THAT DISRUPTS THE FLOW OF MY JASPER!?" "UGH, NOW I HAVE TO CHARGE THEM IN THE MOONLIGHT AGAIN!"

Me: "Oh yea, sorry." "I keep forgetting that your rocks are magic and stuff..." "Man that bra you're wearing rocks!"

* * *

A YEAR INTO OUR RELATIONSHIP, Eliza grew bored of living with me upstate in the Catskills and suggested that we move down to where she was from, so the both of us might better benefit from all of the opportunities one can take advantage of living near the Big Apple, and like the hypnotized simp-pan-zee that I was, I agreed. We vacated our place in Catskill and she went to stay with her sister back in Nassau County while I moved into a spare bedroom at my grandmothers in the Astoria neighborhood of Queens for a while. After all, it was going to be a fiery hot minute before I could afford to live out on Long Island where she wanted to be, (The Paumanok has a section literally called "The Golden Coast", these are the kind of people that do a credit check before renting to you.) and I was not comfortable getting our own place until I had steady work. My uncle was able to set me up with a permanent gig where I used to intern at MTV, making what I called "City Money", and loads of it. I started a savings for us to get our own place again down there, but two weeks into my endeavor she broke things off with me to pursue a gay man she had recently met and insisted she was going to turn him straight if it was the last thing she ever did, leaving me to figure out my next move by myself. "Lol". "What the fuck am I doing down here?"

* * *

THE FIRST WEEKEND AFTER ELIZA left me to pursue someone else, I had to take the Long Island Railroad out to her sister's place so we could practice that time honored tradition of giving each other's stuff back. Eliza had a good cross section of my clothes and comics, and I still had her globe. It was one of her more prized possessions, as each country on it was made of whatever precious stone it was famous for. (Africa was diamonds, China was Jade, etc.) New York is the only city in the world where I feel like you can board a train at Penn Station with a globe on a goddamn cherrywood stand that looked like it belonged in a study, and just sit there with it for a 40 minute journey and have no one bat an eye. When I arrived at her stop for what I hoped would be the final time, I carried the stupid globe across three city blocks to where her sisters house was and knocked on the door. Her sister answered and told me Eliza was upstairs in the bathroom putting on makeup and getting ready to go to an NA meeting. (Eliza was not, nor ever has been a drug addict, she would go to these meetings to meet people who had quote: "Had real life experiences".) Her new trivial pursuit was going to be there tonight so she was applying as much war paint as possible, leaving me standing there waiting on her to just give me back my shit. I felt like a victim of a "droit du seigneur". She finishes and finally gives me back my things just in time for me to catch her new love interest, who looks like a missionary killer, at the door on my way out. At least my stuff is not as cumbersome as a globe, and I am able to cross the three blocks back to the train station without too much trouble. That is until I reached the station, and realized that the next inbound city train isn't coming for another hour and I have to use the restroom direly. I remember that there is a bodega a few blocks up that sold these beers that were brewed in old tequila barrels I used to get all the time and make haste towards it and its potential lavatory. By the time I get up there, things are beyond urgent. I fling the door open and address the cashier.

    Me: "Excuse me, I really really really really need to use your bathroom!" Pius Cashier: "We don't have a public restroom." "I'm sorry!"

    Me: "What!?" "Where do you go then!?" "This is an emergency!" Pius Cashier: "I'm sorry sir, those are the rules."

Me: "Ok, I think I smell what you are stepping in." "HERE!"

I grab the first candy within reach and toss it at her like a ducket at a stripper.

Me: "There, now I am a paying customer!" "Please tell me where your bathroom is!"

Pius Cashier: "IT IS NOT AVAILABLE TO THE PUBLIC!" "NO MATTER WHAT YOU BUY, YOU ARE NOT USING OUR BATHROOM!"

Me: "THANKS FOR THE RECITATION AGAIN LADY" "TELL YOUR PARENTS TO STOP FEEDING YOU AFTER FUCKING MIDNIGHT!"

Pius Cashier: "FUCK YOU ASSHOLE, GET OUT!"

Me: "FUCK ME!?" "YOUR FAMILY TREE IS A WREATH, BITCH!"

I slam the door on my way out, and only make it four paces out the door before I finally lose the fight inside of me due to my rage attack on this woman and shit my pants, right there and then, "hoisted by my own petard" as they say. This day sucks. I walk across the street to a sports bar and ask if I can use the bathroom. Bartender tells me that I need to buy a drink first, so I order a beer. I grab it and head towards the bathroom and lose my soiled pants and boxers and use 400 paper towels that I soak in the sink to get the mess that is the lower half of my body back under control. Luckily I have the clothes that Eliza just gave me back and I switch into those. I search around the bathroom for a garbage can that I can dispose of my old clothes in. Would you believe they did not have one? "Faithless is he that says farewell when the road darkens..." I say as I improvise and stash the soiled garments in a cabinet full of cleaning supplies beneath the restroom sink for someone to find later. I down the beer and head back out into the bar where I tip the guy $15.

Some Apple Knocker Bartender: "Hey, thanks!"

Me: "Oh believe me buddy, you have not earned that yet, but you are gonna later."

* * *

LIKE ALL JILTED YOUNG PERSONS, the first thing that I decided to do to fill the hole in my heart was to start spending lots and lots of my money. After all, the burden of securing a place for myself and Eliza was no longer necessary. I was like a reverse carpetbagger from northern New York trying to help its southern half, going out to bodegas and buying up ready to eat food and giving it out to the homeless on the streets. We didn't have vagrants up in the mountains and seeing them everywhere with little to no options made me realize that my situation was nowhere near as bad as it could be, and I wanted to do something to help others since I felt I could do nothing to help myself at that point. I started purchasing ice cream for this Korean woman named Do-Un who slept on the steps of a church along Lexington Avenue most nights. She had told me she had moved to the states to become a dancer, but accessing that kind of field had proved to be a lot harder than she had expected it to be. Also, she told me she loved American ice cream. "Do-Un to others, am I right!?" I would tell her when I brought her treats, even though I am perfectly certain she did not get the joke. It may even have alarmed her when I said things like that looking back on it now.

* * *

ONE NIGHT, WHILE I WAS ROAMING the city and passing out food to more drifters, my phone rang. It was Christian. He told me that he had a week coming up where he had taken off work to come down and see me for a few days since I had not been back in so long. This was exciting. I had made a few friends while in the city and they were all remarkable people but I longed for the familiarity of the mountains. I needed to cut loose and I had built a false reputation as a respectable man in front of all these cool city kids but I was ready to act a fool and Christain was just the man to do it with.

*　*　*

CHRISTIAN ARRIVED A FEW DAYS later and I promised him a week full of the finest accouterments New York City had to offer. When he first crossed the Triboro Bridge into Astoria, I decided to meet him at the first available block where he could pull over so I could jump in and guide him to my building's parking lot. Christain, not familiar at all with how driving works in the city, took one of my directions a little too literally after I jumped in the car with him, and he interpreted my "first left coming up" as a "turn left immediately, it doesn't even matter if it's possible" which resulted in him plowing his Acura straight into a steel support beam for the Ditmars Boulevard above ground train stop.

Christian: "SHIT!"

Me: "What the fuck was that!?"

Christain: "YOU SAID TO TURN LEFT!"

Me: "WHEN ITS FUCKING POSSIBLE!" "WHAT DID YOU THINK, I WANTED YOU TO PHASE THROUGH TRAFFIC?!" " GET US OUT OF HERE BEFORE THE COPS COME!"

Christian tries to back out and drive off, but the impact from the beam has pressed the front of the cars metal body into a cocoon around the drivers side front tire, heavily restricting its rotation and causing the car to buck forward in rapid spurts which eventually self slashes the tire, blowing it out, and we are forced to pull over into a diner parking lot, only a few yards away. We get out and inspect the damage. The tire is fucked. I sift through Christains trunk and find a metal baseball bat that I use as a pry bar to pull some of the compressed metal away from the tire and freeing its hold upon the pathetic, deflated rubber that brought Christian down here.

Me: "You should be able to get a donut on that and actually drive it now." "Where is your jack?"

Christain: "I have a jack but no donut"

Me: "The hell do you mean, you don't have one?" "The car comes with one!" Christain: "This one did not".

I drop the bat with a hollowed clang on the pavement and start pacing in circles while rubbing my head at this mess. Christain perks up for a moment while I am doing this and starts retrieving more materials from his trunk. A car jack......and a skateboard. I watch in awe as this man pumps the car up with the jack resting on the skateboard.

Christian: "I can probably drive it like this for a short time, the wheels on the skateboard should move the downed corner of the vehicle, though the distribution of its weight upon the board does concern me."

Me: "Are you high!?" "We can't drive through the city like that!" "This isn't some cartoon!" Christain: "You are probably correct, we will have to contact a towing service." "I don't know what I was thinking".

As the words leave his mouth, the car's weight upon the jack finally becomes too much for it to bear on the wooden skateboard, eventually puncturing the boards surface before completely snapping it in half. Christians driver's side sinks back to the ground as his car alarm begins to sound throughout the neighborhood.

* * *

THE NEXT DAY, MYSELF and Christain decided to go explore a long abandoned hall beneath the Brooklyn Bridge, originally used in 1876 to store expensive collections of wine that NY's elite would hoard down there because of the ideal conditions it provided for the grape beveridges, then rented it out much later on in the 1960's as a venue for Andy Warhol's crazy parties. After all, it would be a few hours till his car was fixed at the shop we found online and the spot we were heading to was more easily accessible by subway anyway. After looking over some old maps of Manhattan's subterrania that we ripped off the internet, and some running around the subway tunnels beneath the city's south end, we finally managed to find what was a dark and wet auditorium teeming with rats the size of foxes. Surprisingly there were no homeless shanties in this place, despite its potential. Just scattered trash and rodents upset by our flashlights. Most disappointing was the lack of any old wine racks or priceless works of art in this scary place.

Me: "Well that was a bust..."

Christain: "I don't think I will ever forget the smell of this place so long as I walk this Earth." "It reminds me of handled spare change"

Just then, my phone starts to ring, its tone louder than usual from the acoustics in this filthy cell. It is my DJ buddy from out on the Island, Cassius. Cassius loved to organize shows and played music at multiple venues across Brooklyn, Manhattan, and Long Island. His lovely and sensational girlfriend, Diasha, was in charge of executing the various graphics and special effects they used at these shows. She often would dress for these occasions in a manner I could only describe as "Interstellar Cleopatra". Together they made a very impressive team. The both of them were well known in the electronic dance scene that was resurging in the five boroughs at this time, and probably the both of them rivaled Jake in terms of friendliness and patience.

Me: "Oh here we go, this could be something. I pick up the phone.
Cassius: "Jesse?"
Me: My man!" "What's going on?"
Cassius: "I was calling to see if you wanted to catch a set I'm putting on at a bar in Patchogue tonight?" "I'm trying to fill the place up, can I put you down on the guest list?"
I shine my light over at Christain, who is stooping down now to pick up what looks like a small, white, ping pong ball off of the floor.
Christain: "The party might not be over for old Andy just yet..." He pockets the ball.
Me: "That will be two for the list actually, what time are you going on?

* * *

SEVERAL HOURS LATER and we find ourselves back in the world's borough to pick up Christains Acura, all fixed and ready to leave the lot. I was waiting outside, puffing on a cigarette when he came out of the mechanics office, twirling his car keys.
Christian: "This mechanic really hit a lick with me!" "$350!" "And that's not even including the body work it still needs done!" "This is just so the car will drive!" "Back home I could have had this fixed for less than a third of what this ass ocarina is charging!"
Me: "That's a lot of tuppence".
Christain: "Yeah, your telling me." "How the hell did such a crook come so highly recommended?"
Me: "His family is well connected in this neighborhood, he probably had them all drop those positive reviews we read on the web." "It's all crony capitalism man." "You wanna head back

to my place and get changed, or do you want to show up to this sea of hotties looking like a couple of assholes who were crawling around in the sewers all day?

* * *

WHEN WE GOT BACK to the apartment, the building's doorman, Mateo, let us in with a warm greeting, and we took the elevator to the second floor where I lived. Inside, the both of us switched our attire from cave to rave and then smoked a joint. We had egg rolls for dinner, some real cabbage cannoli's. Back downstairs, we were ready to make our way to the parking lot when Mateo stopped to ask us if we could help him understand something that seemed to have confused and terrified him. He guides our attention to the viewing monitors linked up to the building's security surveillance. After rewinding one of the tapes to a half hour prior, when we were still upstairs getting ready, he asked us to pay close attention to the main lobby's camera. We watch as the tape plays through at normal speed, just Mateo greeting people coming and going from the building, an occasional package drop off, phoning cabs for the tenants, Chinese take-out deliveries, nothing out of the ordinary. But then, he slows the footage down to better focus in on what appears to be a strange, pure white, effervescent orb levitating curiously about the main lobby.

Mateo: "Tell me you both see that?" Christian: "What the fuck..."
Me: "Dude...what was in that joint?"
Mateo clicks the mouse a few times, and the footage moves a little faster. The orb continues to float about the room chaotically with no seeming purpose behind its movements and pulsates like a heartbeat or a drop of water suspended above a high powered fan.

Mateo: ""Have you ever seen anything like that before?"

Christain: "That appears to be an aberration, possibly ectoplasmic in origen" Mateo: "what's your friend here saying?"

Me: "This fool thinks it's a ghost".

Mateo: "HEY!" "Don't say things like that too loud around these parts, these residents get very uncomfortable when you bring up shit like that." "I'm serious, they don't even let us have a 13th floor in most buildings out here." "These blue bloods can be very superstitious". Me: "Mateo, play the tape back at normal speed so I can verify this isnt you fucking with me using a laser pointer."

In truth, I myself could not for the life of me understand what it could possibly be. Mateo gets ready to show us the video at normal speed but briefly clicks the camera onto real time first and ,just then, the orb could be seen once more, flailing about the main lobby, completely directionless like a leaf in the wind. The three of us jumped back and snapped our gaze towards the lobby where the camera picked it up but could see NOTHING with our waking eyes.

Me: "I...I don't understand." "How come the camera can pick it up but our eyes can't!?" Christain: "Try to touch it, see if you can feel a cold spot in the room!"

Me: "....."

Me: "But I can't see it without the camera and it's flying all over the place!"

Mateo: "I can direct you if you want!" "I'll stay in here and watch for it on camera and tell you where it is!"

Let it be said that Jesse James has never shied away from gathering proof of life after death. I walk into the middle of the lobby and await instructions for my Marco Polo match against the spirit.

Mateo: "Oh my god!"

Me: What!?" "What is it!?"

Mateo: "The orb, it's... moving around you, like it's actively trying to avoid you!" Me: "WHAT!?"

Christain: "Jesse!" "It's gone beneath the couch to your immediate right!" "Under the couch!"

I speed walk over to the couch and quickly stab my arm beneath it to feel for the orb's potential chill, but detect nothing. Mateo is now rapidly firing off prayers in Spanish in a low tone, kissing his clenched fist and forming the sign of the cross in front of his person using swift hand gestures which is definitely not good.

Christain: "HOLY SHIT!"

ME: "WHAT!?" "WHAT'S HAPPENING NOW!?"

Christain: "It moved away from you on the camera, like it knew you were lunging for it!" "THAT THING MIGHT BE SENTIENT!"

I stand and march back into the monitor room and demand they rewind the footage so I can see what just happened. Sure enough, when I watch myself root around beneath the couch with my left arm, the orb frantically departs out of sight as if to purposefully elude me.

Christain: "Let's be clear now guys, that is no dust spot on a lens, it avoided Jesse with consideration, which means it can sense us and avoid direct interaction with us if it so chooses."

I could only watch and rewatch the footage in shock. Over and over again. Me: "Mateo, I swear to god, if I find out you are fucking with me somehow..."

But the look of alarm on Mateo's face says it all.

Chrisrtain: "Impossible". "I stood here this entire time and did not witness him using anything to trick you." "Jesse, I believe this to be an authentic anomaly". "The important thing to remember here is that whatever it is, it seemed mindless at first and then displayed some small intelligence when you entered the room with it." "That goes against the rules of "Planck's Constant ```"Particles and waves do not behave in such ways, not even at an atomic scale."

Me: "Mateo, can you download that footage and copy it onto a disk for me?" "I need to bring this to my buddy, Nat, up at MIT." "He needs to see this..."

Mateo: "I am afraid I can't." "Making unauthorized copies of these tapes would violate the privacy standards for the building's tenant's." "The super would kill me".

Me: You have something that might be of great interest to the scientific community, cant you just say "Fuck all that"?

Mateo: "Not when you're in a union kid, I'm sorry." "I got a kid at home I need to think of".

To this day, I am told that the orb returned a handful of times in the weeks following this incident, but the mystery of what it was, where it came from, and even where it went, will always remain unsolved...

* * *

IN THE TIME IT TAKES for me to smoke a single American Spirit, we have completed the hour long drive to Patchogue. When we get there, the guy working the door checks for our names and admits us in with a modest cover. Patchogue is one of those towns that middle aged couples pretend they found by accident and call it things like "our little secret" or "our hidden slice of heaven" and then launch into a prosecco soaked diatribe about all the local shops that you "must visit". Usually to purchase restored antiques or cheeses that give a hint of something no one asked for like catfish or bud light. The inside of the venue looks like a prom at a yacht club. The bar is upscale and has a magnificent selection, Billy Joel would be Strong Island proud of this setting. And the dance floor looks like a carnival, and the microphone smells like a...well it smells like the air that blows out of the back of a PS2.

Cassius is still setting up his tech and wont be going on for another hour so myself and Christain head to the bar and grab some beers. Christain just burned through a good portion of the money he brought down here to fix his car so I picked up the first round. Before long the soon to be rave is teeming with guys and gals dressed with what I think are villains from the Rocketeer universe, as is customary at these things. Lapidarists are peddling their wares, most of which are advertised as "sacred rocks from Woodstock, up in the Catskills' ' that they charge $38 for. I tell Christain that he can make his car repair money back in no time with all the "sacred rocks" I have, lying around my mom's property up in Fish Creek. Down the line from that, are tables set up for tarot readings from a group of honey traps, all sweetly inviting you to explore your fate.

You all know how I feel about this, but Christain took the bait and we both sat down and chose our cards. After my three cards were selected, the Desdemona-esque soothsayer read back to me what the arbitrary Byzantine art of the cards had told her about my past, my present, and my future.

Tarot Reader: "It looks like you are at a crossroads in your life, and are unable to decide which way to go." "But fear not, the answer you seek is with the lion in the mountains' '. Me: "Lady, I don't want to meet any lions out in the mountains." "Where I come from, Catamounts out in the wilds don't give you life advice, they turn you into a carpet of gore."

* * *

O NE OF THE GUYS WHO was in Cassius's crew was holding a beer pong tournament outside on the patio for a cash prize and Christain wanted to sign up. I followed him out and watched him pay his way into the first game. During the tourney's initial round, Christain produced the pong ball that he had scavenged like a rag-n-bone man earlier, in the decadent hall we visited. He proclaimed that the spirit of Andy Warhol was inside that ball, and that it was only appropriate that it was used in the opening shot thrown tonight, and readied to toss it in an arch fashion into the opposing teams cups. But before any of that could happen, the "ball" exploded into millions of baby spiders all over Christains hand and arm in what seemed like an instantaneous act of abiogenesis. He had misidentified a spider's nest full of eggs as a pong ball cobwebbed by age. Christain starts screaming and tearing off his shirt like he's on fire, knocking all of his own teammates cups over in a fit, violently staggering in circles and slapping at his own body, trying to rend the underage arachnids from his own form. For several minutes Christain uses exaggerated, patterned movements to remove all the spiders like a silly rube goldberg machine. Finally he feels safe enough to put his shirt back on (After he flapped it out a few times with both hands in front of him, just in case.)and tried to continue the game, but he is told that because he knocked over all his own cups that he to either had to buy more or forfeit. I cover the bill for his new beers and head back inside to catch Cassius's set which is now just starting to come on. Diasha steps out onto the stage, addressing the crowd like a chanteuse and dressed just as fashionably. She introduces Cassius and he wastes no time filling the house with his hard style. A mixture of sounds like you are scoring points in an older video game and an alternative version of Fantasia that was orchestrated in Hell. The crowd loves it, and I even find myself dancing for a bit. I forget who it was that said, "I don't know much about art, but I know what I like."

* * *

A FEW HOURS GO BY AND the party's over. Myself and Christain find each other out on the dance floor when the lights come back on. I don't know what happened with him and that drinking game, but it looked like he had been dancing for almost as long as I had been.

Me: "What did I tell ya!?" "Great time, or what?"

Christain: "Jesse, one of your compatriots from outside was nice enough to offer me to partake in an MDMA derivative earlier." "Coupled with the dancing I believe I am having some sort of religious experience and do not wish to conclude our night just yet."

Me: "You mean you're rolling?" "Hahahahahaha" "Ok, what do you want to do?" Christain: "I wish to traverse the entirety of this island before sunrise." "Till we can go no further."

Me: "You mean Montauk?" "You want to go to Montauk all the way out in the Hamptons?" Christain: "According to my phone's navigations, the journey would only take us an hour and 20 minutes depending on traffic, which I suspect will be light given that the hour is late". "Also I am afraid my body will not be responsive to any relaxing techniques utilized to achieve somnolence at this time."

Me: "Yeah, I get it." "Your fucking wired and you wanna take a long drive." "Alright, I am all for pushing this night as far as it can go." "Let's hit it...."

* * *

A LONG THE WAY, I HAD Christain pull off at a 24 hour supermarket in Eastern Suffolk off the Sunrise Highway.The town is all industrial and depressing like a place Bruce Springsteen would sing about.Thank god we are not here for long. I led him to the seafood deli and started filling a bag with fresh fish.

Christain: "What is all this for?"

Me: "We're going to make chum with it." Christain: "Chum?" "Why chum?"

Me: "To bring sharks." "Sharks hunt at night, and I want to see some, that's why the chum" "I told you we were going to push this night as far as we could."

I go behind the deli counter since no one is there to stop me and discover a large hooked blade that reminds me of an Egyptian khopesh. I use it to pestle my fish into a bucket of bloody chunks that smells just fucking awful.

Christain: "I think what you are talking about is commonly referred to as blood baiting and could be considered extremely dangerous to the inexperienced."

EPILOGUE

"THE END"

MONTAUK IS A HAMLET in the East Hamptons that most New Yorkers refer to as "THE END". Which is fitting because that is the part of the book that we have now come to. Montauk got the nickname "THE END" because the island quite literally ends and becomes the open ocean. Christain did indeed drive through the night as he said he would until we reached Montauk Point and he parked his car at the base of the lighthouse there. We both exited the vehicle and made our way down to the beach and into the surf of the dark Atlantic. We only go out far enough to where it is ankle deep before I start slapping handfuls of fish viscera from my bucket into the now receding tide. Christains is still under the thrall of the molly, and his brain is firing off electrical signals around his neurons like a Parkinson's patient trying to aim a roman candle.

Me: "You know Christain, I had a really great time with you this week." Christain: "It has been both recreationally satisfying and educational Jesse."

I pitch another handful of fish gore, this time a few more yards out. I have taken notice that these chunks do not sink and float towards the surface. I keep hoping I will see the sinister dorsal fin of a hammerhead or a bull shark skate across the waves and take the bait like colony insects hauling off their dead for necrophoresis. As I stood there, trying to lure apex predators so old and formidable that their ancestors survived the KT extinction and Christain dances to songs that only he can hear, I suddenly became aware of how happy I have been since his arrival. Things seemed more harmonious, more natural, like a part of me I had left upstate had come down with him and found its way back to me. It was empowering. The enemy of anxiety is routine. All that is familiar was mine to control, it could not take me by surprise or scare me, because I already knew how it all turned out in the end.

I had come down here for all the wrong reasons. To make Eliza happy. And now Eliza is gone. And where did that leave me? What was I still doing here? I was not happy, but I wanted to be, and now I knew how. Life is not a training session, it is the title bout. The waves were starting to come in higher now and washed over our knees, pulling whatever it was that kept me downstate for all these years out of me, and back out with it to sea.

Me: "I'm going back with you tomorrow when you leave for upstate."
Christian: "When did you decide this?"

The drugs make him speak as if he possesses the knowledge of all the ages of this world. He does not seem in the slightest bit surprised by my sudden want for an immediate departure from a life I spent three years building for myself down here.

Me: "Just now". "After all this, I have come to "THE END", Christain." "I can go no further here". "Whatever I came down here for no longer matters". "This was never my home, I just pretended it was". "I don't belong down here in a place like this". "I miss the Catskills". I never wanted to be a posh citiot, you know the kind of guy with enough money to do something twice but never enough to do it the right way, anyhow." "That's not me." "That's not who I am."

* * *

THE NEXT DAY, Christain started us on the road back upstate before I even woke up. While I was sleeping, Christain had successfully navigated us back across Long Island to Queens and over the bridge into the Bronx, and even got us lost briefly in Connecticut.

When I finally did sit up we were crossing the Tappan Zee Bridge over to Rockland County listening to some god awful emo station. (White male sympathy was a rough time for music.) It was not long before I could see the rolling hills of the Catskills peeking out from beyond the town of Ulster. Christain pulls off at the Saugerties exit so I can hop out at the Stewarts across from it.

He still has a long journey ahead of him back to his apartment in Albany, so it is here that we go our separate ways. I had texted my mother earlier and asked her if she could pick me up from there. My mother is a very sweet person in an anachronistic way. Deborah Angelino's kindness was something from before this time. I have non figuratively watched my mother give someone the shirt off of her very own back before, and then get a ticket for indecent exposure as a direct result.

The funny part is, my mother was already at the gas station before I even arrived, buying multiple gallons of milk for the house. Something I noticed her mother always did too. I really had to pee so I told her that I was going to use the restroom while she was in line with a cow's worth of dairy. The door to the bathroom was locked by somebody already inside so I tried to wait, but as the minutes rolled by and this dude was still posted up in there, my mothers legendary kindness began to fade. She had already purchased her things and had come over to see what was taking me so long.

It has been a long time since I had been back upstate to visit her and she is thrilled that I have asked to move back in with her for a while till I get on my feet.

Deborah: "How long has this guy been in there?"

Me: "Like, 12 minutes." "Maybe I can just pee behind the building."

Deborah: "12 minutes!?"

She starts banging on the door with her free fist.

Deborah: "WHAT ARE YOU DOING IN THERE!?" "IT'S A STEWARTS BATHROOM, NOT A FUCKING AIR B-N-B!" "LETS GO!"

Everyone in the store has stopped to look at us. Me: "Mom...please stop."

From inside the bathroom we can all hear the toilet flush. Then strangely flush again and then again..

Me: "Why is he flushing so much?

Deborah: "IT'S AN OLD TRICK TO COVER UP THE SOUND OF SNORTING COKE!" Me: "WHAT!?"

Deborah: "Oh yeah, the guys at studio 54 used to do that shit all the time back in the day, let me tell ya!"

Finally the door opens and a nervous looking heavy set fellow comes out and bolts past me and my loud mom. It was good to be back.

Unbeknownst to me at the time, this embarrassing interaction would bring me the end game love and stability I had long searched for.

ACKNOWLEDGEMENTS

I WANT TO START BY THANKING my English professor at SUNY Ulster, Penny Rifenburgh for showing how to write this, not to mention encouraging me to.

Jordan and the rest of the staff at the Saugerties Public Library, thank you for taking the time to show me how to use practically every digital writing application correctly so I could ACTUALLY write this.

My Mom, Deborah Angelino who thinks this is going to be the next Hemmingway and will shit when she reads all these stories I never told her.

Web Beveridge for his wisdom, without which I would not have arrived at a place in my life where I would write a book.

Nathaniel and Holli Galloway for letting me use their home PC for sometimes upwards of eight hours to keep writing this, long after the library doors would close.

Zachary Coons for the photography on the cover.

My Brother, Chase Hinchey and his girlfriend Alexa Prochaska for letting me read some of these stories aloud to them so I could try them out.

Rachel Byrne, for editing this entire book, and for ceaselessly encouraging me to write, and for not letting me give up.

JESSE ANGELINO was born in midtown Manhattan, and was raised in Palenville, NY in the great northern Catskill Mountains, between the townships of Catskill and Saugerties. He enjoys creative writing, cooking spicy food, hiking in the mountains, and playing games of science with his daughter, Lily.

www.ingramcontent.com/pod-product-compliance
Lightning Source LLC
LaVergne TN
LVHW011728060526
838200LV00051B/3071